"I need a competent girl Friday."

Andros went on to explain. "Someone to run things in the tower at Vathia while I'm working on my book."

"You mean you want me to live with you?" Jess asked incredulously.

"Of course this would be strictly a business relationship," he added.

"How do I know you're not some kind of loony who'll rape me the moment you get me alone?" Jess demanded.

He smiled. "You'll just have to take my word that, if the lady's unwilling, I'm not about to force myself on her."

"I can assure you I'm not in the least willing," she replied. "I don't want to be rude...." She crossed her feet. Somewhere she'd read that if you crossed your feet while you told a lie, you wouldn't be found out. "But you're simply not my type."

Celia Scott, originally from England, came to Canada for a vacation and began an "instant love affair" with the country. She started out in acting but liked romance fiction and was encouraged to make writing her career when her husband gave her a typewriter as a wedding present. She now finds writing infinitely more creative than acting since she gets to act out all her characters' roles, and direct, too.

Books by Celia Scott

HARLEQUIN ROMANCE
2568—SEEDS OF APRIL
2638—STARFIRE
2735—WHERE THE GODS DWELL
2831—A TALENT FOR LOVING

Catch a Dream

Celia Scott

Harlequin Books

TORONTO • NEW YORK • LONDON
AMSTERDAM • PARIS • SYDNEY • HAMBURG
STOCKHOLM • ATHENS • TOKYO • MILAN

Original hardcover edition published in 1988
by Mills & Boon Limited

ISBN 0-373-02945-4

Harlequin Romance first edition November 1988

CHAPTER ONE

IT WAS late afternoon when the bus dropped the two English girls in the small town of Yerolimin, the end of the bus line and a few kilometres from the village of Vathia. Jess Firbank stretched her long legs and looked around her. The town consisted of little more than two hotels and a dramatic wall of rock, rising sheer from the far end of the little beach. Inland, the rocky heights of the Taiyetos mountains soared into the sky.

'It's so hot!' moaned Kitty.

'It usually is in Greece.' Rather wearily, Jess pushed a strand of toffee-coloured hair out of her eyes. Kitty had done nothing but complain since they'd left Gatwick early that morning. Jess was just as hot and tired as her young cousin, and it would have been heaven to take a swim in the crystal-clear water that lapped the little beach, and then have a cool drink at one of the two *tavernas* on the quayside. But this was no pleasure trip. 'We'd better get going,' Jess insisted. 'It's no good standing around here feeling sorry for ourselves.'

Kitty looked sidelong at her cousin's face and decided not to voice the protest that sprang to her lips. Jess's usually smiling grey eyes were hard with determination, as they had been ever since they had embarked on this quest. 'Do we have to look for Andros straight away? I'd rather...'

'Yes, we do. I have to be back at work on Monday, remember? Unless you're prepared to face this man on your own——' Jess broke off as she stared at Kitty's pretty, woebegone face. She would be no match for Andros Kalimantis; only two years younger than Jess,

5

she was far younger in common sense. She would be reduced to a whimpering heap in no time flat. Look at her now, a pathetic kitten of a girl with no fight in her.

She remembered Kitty's distress when, only a few days ago, she had come looking for Jess at the pub in Brighton where she worked. It had been nearly closing time at the Saracen's Head, and as usual the place was crowded, everyone jostling up to the bar to place their final orders before the barman called, "Time." Jess had only worked at the pub for six weeks, but already she was fairly popular with the regulars. People liked to be served by someone pleasant and competent, and the fact that she was also a very pretty girl with a wealth of dark blonde hair didn't hurt, either. The regulars thought Ted and Ann Purvis were lucky to have her as their barmaid, and the Purvises agreed.

Jess had supported herself since leaving school, doing all sorts of jobs: waitressing, clerical work...but this was her first stint at working in a pub. It was fun. Even when she was as rushed as she was tonight it was fun. But, at twenty-three, she'd decided she wanted more out of life than standing behind a bar, handing out drinks. Somehow, she was going to save enough from her salary to take a business management course, and qualify for the kind of job that would offer her some sort of stability. Because stability was a commodity she'd been short of all her life.

It wasn't until Ted nudged her and pointed that Jess became aware of her young cousin standing at the crowded bar.

'Hello, Kit-Kat, are you by yourself?' Usually Kitty was with her steady boyfriend, Charlie.

'Jess, I *must* talk to you.' Kitty's voice sounded shaky, and Jess noticed that her eyelids were puffy and red. Oh dear, thought Jess, trouble! The two girls were not particularly close, but Kitty had always relied on Jess for a shoulder to cry on. And Jess always supplied it. Kitty might irritate her sometimes, so that Jess longed to shake her until she rattled, but she always helped. And it was obvious that help was going to be needed.

'You'll have to wait until closing time, Kitty. Find a seat somewhere. I'll be as quick as I can.'

'All right.' Kitty meekly took the bottle of tonic water Jess handed her. 'I'll go and sit over by the door.'

It was ten minutes before Ted Purvis started ringing the bronze ship's bell to signal closing time, and meanwhile Jess was too busy even to speculate what Kitty's problem might be. It must be something to do with the absent Charlie, Jess decided. Her cousin was so *gullible*. They shared similar backgrounds, but Kitty had never learned any caution regarding that treacherous emotion called love. Love, to Jess, was nothing but a four-letter word; her mother, and her mother's sister, had been sobering examples of what it could do.

At last the groups of customers began breaking up and heading for the door, good-naturedly complaining that Ted's clock was fast. When the place was empty, Jess hurried through her chores, only taking time to pull a comb through her hair and apply a touch of lip-gloss before collecting Kitty. As they went out into the soft June night, Jess asked whether her cousin would need a bed for the night; Kitty sometimes chose to stay on the sofa in Jess's bed-sitting-room rather than travelling back to her flat in London. Kitty winced.

'No, I—I don't need——'

Tears were threatening. 'Let's go to the coffee-bar near the station, then,' Jess said diplomatically. 'Then you won't have to rush for your train. You can tell me what the trouble is first, and then cry.' Whatever it was, it couldn't be all that bad, she thought. Past experience had taught her that Kitty was prone to self-dramatisation. But, as she was to discover when they were established at a table and the waitress had brought their coffee, she was wrong.

'Oh, Jess! I'm in the most terrible trouble,' gulped Kitty, dabbing at her pale cheeks with a wodge of tissue. 'I'm...I'm...going to have a baby.'

'Oh darling!' Appalled, Jess put her slender hand over Kitty's plump one. 'Don't cry, Kit-Kat. You know Charlie loves you, he'll stand by you. Have you told him yet?'

The younger girl withdrew her hand as the colour crept into her face. 'Charlie's gone back to Australia,' she said in a voice barely above a whisper.

'Well, there are things called *phones*,' her cousin pointed out. 'You must tell him right away.'

'It's got nothing to do with Charlie.' Kitty played with a strand of her hair. 'It's not Charlie's baby.'

'I see.' Jess tried not to sound dismayed. 'Whose is it?'

'A man I met after Charlie left. A Greek.' She raised her eyes and looked full into Jess's steady grey ones. 'Oh, Jess! He was so wonderful...so handsome! I met him at a party...and I was feeling so down about Charlie...Andros just swept me off my feet...'

'And into his bed.'

'Oh! I know it sounds like that,' Kitty protested, 'but it wasn't really. He said he loved me, and he did such romantic things...'

'Obviously.'

'No...it wasn't *like* that, I tell you! We fell madly in love. We couldn't help ourselves...'

'Spare me the details,' Jess interrupted. 'Have you told *him*?'

'I couldn't,' Kitty's childish lips trembled. 'I don't know where to get in touch with him.'

Jess took a sip of coffee. 'I see. It was a one-night affair, then?'

'*No!* I keep telling you...he said he loved me. We saw each other every day for a month.'

'And in all that time you never asked him where he *lived*?'

'Of course I did. He lived in Athens...he said. His office was in Athens, and I wrote to him there. But...' the tears rose again '...but my letters were all returned unopened. And then I saw this in tonight's paper.' She fumbled in her bag, brought out a piece of torn newsprint and handed it to Jess.

It was a small item from a gossip column which read, 'Well known London businessman Andros Kalimantis has flown to his Grecian hideaway in the village of Vathia. He has buried himself in this remote part of the Peloponnese in order to take a much needed holiday, and to search for material for a possible book. Knowing this eligible bachelor's popularity with the fair sex, our writer wonders if Mr Kalimantis will spend the summer alone!'

'It says *London* businessman,' Jess said as she passed the cutting back.

'I *know*,' wailed Kitty, 'I don't understand it, he told me he lived in Greece and he was just here on business.'

'He certainly was,' Jess agreed drily. 'When is this baby due?' And then, remembering how scatty Kitty was, she asked, 'Have you seen a doctor? I mean, you are *sure*?'

Kitty was indignant. 'Of course I'm sure! The baby's due in about seven months. *And* I get dreadfully sick in the morning,' she added as a clincher.

'Well,' Jess pushed her unfinished coffee aside, 'the first thing we must do is find you a good solicitor. This Andros must help you financially, Kitty, that's only right.'

'I don't want to hound Andros about money,' Kitty protested. 'He *loves* me. And when he knows I'm having his child he'll want to marry me.'

Jess looked grim. 'Even supposing he does, he's obviously lied to you, and according to that news item he's a womaniser, too. Do you *want* to marry a man like that?'

But Kitty was adamant. 'I'll have to go to this village and find him, Jess,' she insisted, 'and you must come with me.'

Jess argued, but she could feel the clutch of doom. Once again she was going to have to help Kitty sort out her problems, as she had done so often before. It would mean breaking a date with a nice man she'd just met, but it couldn't be helped; Kitty needed her, and she couldn't find it in her heart to let her down.

Smiling mistily, her cousin told her that she was an angel. 'I don't know what I'd do without you, Jess. Ever since Mummy died...'

Jess, who privately believed that her aunt Mary had always been useless as a mother, merely patted her little cousin's arm and said, 'Forget it! You'd do the same for me,' although she wasn't entirely sure about that.

Jess had been five when her father died, and her mother, Angela, had remarried two years later. It had not been a success, and when Jess was eleven there had been a bitter divorce. Jess knew just *how* bitter, because her mother took her out of the boarding school where she had been happy and brought her home: Angela needed a sympathetic ear and, because Kitty's mother was in the midst of her own marital problems, Jess was expected to supply it. Wide grey eyes sombre, Jess had listened while Angela cried and told her how all her dreams of love had turned to ashes. 'We were so happy at the beginning,' her mother had sobbed, 'I was sure it would last for ever.'

By the time Jess entered her teens, she was convinced that love was an illusion and that the chances of making a happy marriage were nil. There were plenty of men in her life, for she was warm-hearted and fun, but as soon as a man became serious she backed off. She wasn't going to risk the kind of disillusionment her mother and her aunt had put themselves through. Not for anyone in the world!

And now, it seemed, Kitty had managed to break her heart without even getting as far as the altar. And here *she* was, spending her precious weekend and most of her precious savings, looking for Andros Kalimantis, to break the news that he was going to be a father!

They found the only taxi in the village, and with the help of her phrase-book Jess managed to tell the driver where they wanted to go. After refusing the driver's gallant offer to ride beside him, she climbed in the back with Kitty, and with a squeal of tyres they left the main street and headed inland.

Many people would have found the rocky landscape forbidding, but Jess liked it. It was uncompromising, and that appealed to her. She glanced back at the foothills. They were like verdant pasture land compared to this hostile terrain, where the only plants that seemed to flourish were cactus and olive trees.

The driver said something and pointed ahead to a wide ridge that was jagged with broken towers like a dragon's spine. 'Vathia,' he said with much grinning and head shaking. 'Vathia, ne!'

Jess's grey eyes widened, for as she gazed ahead she could see a small army of towers that seemed to lie on the steep bluff like chess pieces thrown on to the mountainside.

'What an incredible place.' She turned to Kitty. 'Didn't your Andros ever tell you about it?'

Kitty shook her head. 'I think it's ghastly,' she said. 'It's nothing but a pile of old stones.' Her face was sullen, so Jess kept quiet. No point trying to explain that the gaunt beauty of the place captured her imagination. She had never been to the Peloponnese, but had taken a holiday once in Greece, and had fallen totally under the spell of the place. Its landscape and its history struck a responsive chord in her, and she had again felt a quickening of her pulse when their plane had touched down in Athens.

By now they had approached the cluster of towers, and the taxi turned along a road that was edged with a bulbous jungle of prickly pear. They drove into a small square, where a few motionless mulberry trees stood beside a small taverna. At the tables placed strategically in the shade, some old men sat nursing their glasses. They stared unblinkingly at the two blonde girls.

Jess handed some drachmas to the driver and watched as the car disappeared. She had a moment's concern, wondering how they would get back to Yerolimin, but decided to worry about that later. Right now, they had to find Kitty's lover.

An old woman—everyone seemed to be old in this place—came out from the taverna and examined the two visitors. Her wrinkled face was not exactly welcoming, but nevertheless Jess smiled warmly and tried out her Greek. At the name Kalimantis, the woman's face re-laxed a little and she pointed to a tower, larger than the others, that was built on a promontory of rock about half a mile from the village. 'Kalimantis!' she nodded, 'Kalimantis...there.'

'It looks as if we've found him,' Jess said, but Kitty didn't seem too happy at the news.

'Oh, Jess! I do feel such a wreck,' she whimpered. 'Do you think there's a loo here, where I could wash?'

Jess peered doubtfully into the dim room that was little more than a shack. 'I doubt it.' Looking up the word for 'wash' in her phrase-book, she tried it out on the old woman, who pointed a gnarled finger at a pump at the corner of the square.

'That's the wash and brush-up,' she told Kitty, 'and I suspect there's an outdoor loo at the back of the taverna.'

'Oh, my God!' Kitty shuddered visibly.

'Let's have a cold drink here first,' Jess suggested. 'After all, we can't very well use the facilities without patronising the place.' She steered her cousin to a table and ordered two lemonades, which the old woman produced from a large refrigerator—an incongruous modern item which stood outside the building.

'We mustn't linger,' Jess warned when Kitty pushed aside her drink after one sip, 'it will be dark soon. I don't fancy trying to find that tower in the dark.'

'Oh, Jess! I can't,' Kitty quavered, her blue eyes filling with tears.

'What do you mean?' said Jess, her hand raised in the act of tucking a loose hairpin back into the knot of her French-braided hair.

The tears spilled from Kitty's brimming eyes. 'Don't be angry, Jess,' she pleaded. 'But I look so *awful*...if Andros sees me looking like this...'

'So what? It's his fault if you look a mess,' said Jess, jabbing in pins. 'If he loves you, he'll understand.'

'He *won't*!' the younger girl cried. 'He doesn't like women to look a mess...and besides, I don't feel well. I don't think I can walk a step.'

She *was* pale...and she was pregnant...and they'd been travelling since early morning. It would be disastrous if she became ill in such an out-of-the-way place. 'Will you be all right just sitting quietly here?' Jess asked. 'I'll bring him to you.'

Kitty's wan face lit up. 'Oh, Jess! *Would* you?'

'I just hope he's in,' Jess muttered, picking up her bag. 'I want to get this business over with.'

'Tell him I love him,' Kitty quavered, and over her shoulder Jess said,

'I'll tell him a great deal more than that!'

But Kitty cried out, 'Don't tell him about the baby. I want to tell him that myself.'

Jess washed her face and hands at the pump before setting off. This morning at Gatwick she'd felt quite smart in a green wrap skirt and pink cotton shirt, but now she felt travel-stained and wrinkled. Well, to hell with it! She was here to see Kitty got justice, not impress her paramour.

It took about fifteen minutes to reach the tower. The village was a bewildering maze of cobbled streets, and the place seemed completely deserted. Yet there were signs of life: a scythe leaning against an iron studded door, a cat stretched asleep on a wall.

When she reached the jutting crag of rock, she saw there was a car parked beside the walled yard at the foot of the tower. Thank God! It looked as if someone was around.

She walked into the yard and approached the low front entrance of the tower. The door was propped open and, after looking in vain for a door-knocker or bell, she banged with her fist and called out, 'Hello! Anybody home?'

Her voice sounded thin in the evening stillness. There was no answer and she stepped inside. All she could see was a soot-blackened empty fireplace, over which hung an immense black iron cauldron and a ladder, leaning at a steep angle against a trapdoor. She called again. Her voice echoed eerily against the thick walls of the tower. A shiver of apprehension went through her, and she backed out into the yard again.

The evening sunlight resembled faded cloth of gold, and the silent village of towers had a dreamlike quality. She had the sensation of being caught in a time warp, and if a medieval knight in full armour had appeared she wouldn't have been surprised; so when a deep male voice, very much alive and undreamlike, called from the top of the tower, she nearly jumped out of her skin.

'Who the hell is that?' demanded the voice again. Tilting her head, Jess saw a face peering down at her. It was too dim now to make out more than a shock of black hair and a dark moustache.

'I'm looking for Andros Kalimantis,' she barked back.

'What for?' said the man at the top of the tower. He leaned further over the edge and she noticed how dark his skin was against his white shirt.

'I have a message for him.'

'What is it?'

'I have to give it to him personally,' she shouted irritably. 'Is he there?'

'You'd better come up,' said the man, adding, 'and bring a glass. You'll find one by the sink.'

The man disappeared, so she went back into the dark kitchen and started to climb up the ladder. She didn't even *try* to find the sink, let alone a glass. She was damned if she was taking orders from this man, whoever he was. If he wanted a glass, let him fetch it for himself!

It was a very odd experience, climbing, storey after storey, to the top of the tower. Like climbing up the inside of an enormous chimney. Jess caught ghostly glimpses of furniture on each floor. Armchairs and sofa on the first floor, a bed on the second. On the third there was a desk and a quantity of boxes strewn about on the floor. The last floor seemed only to contain packing cases which looked horribly like coffins in the gloom.

She was out of breath when she reached the roof, but it was worth the climb, for the sky, which was now the colour of lavender silk, was vaulted above her, and the air was cool and sweet. The roof was about eight yards square, surrounded by a low parapet, and the man who had yelled down to her was sitting on this, his back to the mountains, so his face was lit by the setting sun.

He was dark as a gypsy, with eyes that glittered, and curly black hair that fell untidily over his wide forehead. A thick black moustache covered his top lip. He was wearing khaki shorts which were frayed and crumpled, and a pair of very scuffed thonged sandals were on his bare feet. He looked big and muscular and seemed to Jess to exude an aura of dangerous vitality. She wondered for a moment if she was safe up here with him. It was too high to jump, and it was doubtful anyone would hear—or care—if she screamed.

'Now,' he said, 'what's all this about?'

His voice was the next surprise, for out of this Greek ruffian came an English accent as mellow as a BBC announcer's.

'Are *you* Andros Kalimantis?' asked Jess.

'That's me!' He looked at her more closely. 'Didn't you bring that glass?'

'No, I didn't.' Then she asked, 'Are you really Andros Kalimantis?' because he didn't look remotely the way Kitty had described him.

'You don't sound convinced.' He rose to his feet. He was very tall, over six feet, which was unusual in this part of the world.

'It's been a long day,' she said.

'Never mind. I'll fetch you a glass and you can join me in an ouzo.'

'I don't want a drink, thank you,' she said, but he had already started down the ladder.

Jess went to the parapet. A scattering of lights lay along the coast, like glow-worms. Her toe stubbed against something heavy and looking down she saw a heap of iron cannon balls. *Cannon balls?* She knelt to make quite sure she wasn't hallucinating. She wasn't; they were cannon balls all right—pitted with age and piled into a small pyramid.

'Here we are,' said Andros Kalimantis, climbing back on to the roof. He produced a tumbler and went to a small tin table where a bottle, a pottery jug, and a twin to the glass he carried stood. 'The water may not be very cold by now, but we'll have to make do. I don't feel like making another trek to the pump.'

'I don't want a drink,' Jess told him again.

'Will you force me to drink alone?' He smiled disarmingly, but Jess was having none of it.

'You were drinking alone when I got here,' she said.

He nodded. 'True. Besides, I've been slaving away all day on plumbing, I'm thirsty.' He poured a healthy tot for himself and added a splash of water. He raised his glass, which was now the colour of skimmed milk. 'Cheers!'

'I thought you were supposed to be Greek,' said Jess.

'Half-Greek. My Mama is British.'

'You didn't tell Kitty any of this,' Jess accused him.

If she had hoped for a reaction at the mention of Kitty's name, she was disappointed, for all he said was, 'What are you? The census taker?'

Striking a match on the rough stone wall, he lit a lantern and placed it in the centre of the little table. His face was thrown into sudden relief and now Jess could see that his eyes were as black as jet and his hair was so dark it looked purple in the lamplight.

'You know a great deal about me,' he said. 'I think it's time you told me who *you* are.' He looked at her appraisingly and seated himself beside her. 'It's not often beautiful blondes come visiting. Are you sure you're not a nereid come to carry me off to your waterside haunt?'

Jess moved a millimetre away from him. His closeness disturbed her, and now he was starting to chat her up. Playing his role of lady-killer to the hilt, damn him! She became uncharacteristically prim. 'I'm Kitty Taylor's cousin,' she said sternly, fixing him with a hard stare.

'Are you now?' He regarded her cheerfully. 'And do you have a name as well?'

She did not return his smile. 'I'm Jessica Firbank,' she said, and then added, 'Aren't you interested in hearing about Kitty at all?'

'I'm *fascinated*,' he drawled. Stung by his sarcasm, she said sharply, 'You should be. You have a responsibility to Kitty. But you strike me as the type who takes his fun and runs.'

'You sound like a bad Victorian novel,' he mocked, but the fun had gone out of his voice and he eyed her with sudden suspicion.

'I haven't come all this way to trade insults.' She took a step away and the lamplight gleamed on her barley-corn hair. 'Kitty is waiting at the taverna now,' she told him.

'The taverna. Here in Vathia?' She nodded. 'And you think I should see her?'

'I think you owe her that, at least.'

'*Do* I, indeed?' He stared back insolently through hooded eyes.

'Let me tell you something, Mr. Kalimantis.' Jess's cheeks were hot with indignation. 'Kitty may think you're the answer to a maiden's prayer, but as far as I'm concerned you're nothing but bad news!'

'But Kitty thinks I'm the answer to a maiden's prayer, does she?'

'She thinks you're God's gift.' Her lip curled derisively. 'Frankly, I wouldn't take you free with a packet of soap powder!'

A muscle twitched in his cheek. Going to the table, he poured some more water into his drink, and she noticed that he had the same sensuous kind of mouth she'd admired on some of the Greek statues she had seen. And about as much heart as a statue too, she thought bitterly.

'Before we drop in on Kitty,' he said, 'I intend to finish my drink. So you might as well take that scowl off your face.'

'Never mind my face,' said Jess, 'it's Kitty you should be thinking about.'

'Possibly. But a few more minutes might give you time to mend your manners.' He was no longer attempting to charm her, and for a moment she was sorry. It would have been nice to have met under different circumstances. Flirting with him would have been fun.

'You've spoilt the sunset; I don't intend to let you spoil my pre-dinner drink as well,' he said.

More than his pre-dinner drink would be spoilt when Kitty had given him her news, Jess thought malevolently. But she was worried. Now that she had met him, she was more concerned for her cousin than ever. This macho Greek—or Englishman, or whatever he was— would bring a girl like Kitty nothing but unhappiness.

'Do you intend to go on standing there like a pillar of salt?' he asked. He had returned to his seat on the parapet and was unhurriedly sipping his drink.

'I intend to wait here until you pry yourself loose and come with me to Kitty,' Jess informed him.

His brows rose. 'Such solicitude is quite unnecessary. I can find my own way to the taverna.' He gave her a dismissive nod, but she stood her ground.

'Oh, no! I saw that car of yours parked outside. You could do a bunk in no time flat.'

'I'm not in the habit of running away,' he said, his voice cold.

'I happen to think sending back letters unopened is a kind of running away,' retorted Jess.

'Letters?' he questioned.

Jess's temper exploded. 'Oh, stop being so hypocritical!' she flashed. 'Try not to be more of a louse than you are.'

'And why don't *you* stop being so damned self-righteous?' he suggested, draining his glass. 'It doesn't become you.'

'That's a standard response from men who use women as sex objects.' She looked down at her clenched hands. She was beginning to really hate him, because he was making her sound like a Mrs Grundy, and she wasn't a bit like that. She'd always had a policy of live and let live. As long as people didn't hurt others, Jess believed you should mind your own business. But Kitty *was* hurt, and the man who'd hurt her didn't seem to give a tinker's curse.

Turning his glass around in his strong brown hand, he asked, 'What's *your* interest in all this? Where do you fit in?'

'I've told you. I'm her cousin. I'm the only relative she has in the world,' she said, although technically she supposed her mother was closer. Wasn't an aunt closer than cousin? But that was irrelevant, since Jess's mother lived in America, and in any case Angela Newton wasn't the type to take much interest in other people's troubles.

'You can cut out the pathos,' he said disdainfully, 'it doesn't cut any ice with me.'

'I can believe *that*. I don't think you have any heart at all.'

That he could be so contemptuous of silly, gullible Kitty filled her with rage. If he had toppled off his perch on the parapet and crashed to the yard below she would have cheered!

'I think you've done enough play-acting,' he said, putting his empty glass and the contents of the table into a basket that stood in the shadows. He lowered it over the side of the tower, paying out a rope that was tied to the handle. When it reached the ground, he threw the rope after it. 'I think it's time we stopped parrying.' He towered over her, a black-haired giant, and again she felt a frisson of fear. 'Let's go to the taverna and get things straightened out.'

She said, with all the dignity she could muster, 'That's what I've been asking you to do for the past ten minutes!'

However, he ignored her and, going to the trapdoor, said, 'Let me go first, then, if you fall, you can fall on me.'

When the top of his raven head had disappeared, she started down with him just below her. She was conscious of showing a great deal of smooth gold thigh, because her wraparound skirt gaped when she climbed.

Back in the kitchen, he picked up a torch from the wooden dresser and silently held the front door open before ducking out after her, then he grasped her arm tightly above the elbow and switched on the torch. 'Watch your step,' he said, 'the ground's uneven.'

She tried unsuccessfully to remove herself from his grip. She had the uncomfortable feeling that he was taking command of the situation, and she wasn't happy about that. She was finding it increasingly difficult to reconcile this man with the glowing description Kitty had painted. 'He's so handsome,' Kitty had enthused, 'like a film star.' Jess would never have described him this way. A pirate—yes. A thug! But never Robert Redford! There was a dark, menacing quality that sat oddly with his cultured British accent, but it was a menace that was sexy. Oh, he was sexy all right! But although Kitty was pretty, surely she wasn't his type? Why, seducing Kitty would be like shooting fish in a barrel to a man like this. Unsportsmanlike. Silly little Kitty was a walking target, and the man who had shot her down had to be an unscrupulous bastard!

They reached the square and Andros switched off the torch. Kitty was sitting with her back to them, her silvery curls glistening in the taverna's light. Jess stole a quick glance into the face of the big man by her side, but his expression was unreadable. Softly, she called her cousin's name, and Kitty drew her breath in sharply and half turned.

'I brought him, Kitty,' said Jess.

Andros Kalimantis gave a mocking bow. 'Kitty, I presume,' and Jess was about to protest when she caught sight of her cousin's face.

Kitty's blue eyes were stretched wide. 'Who is this, Jess?' she asked.

It's the strain, thought Jess; she's starting to crack-up. 'It's Andros,' she said gently.

'It's not!' Kitty squealed. 'It's *not*! I've never seen this man before in my life!'

CHAPTER TWO

THERE was a silence and everyone in the taverna stared at them.

'You *said* you were Andros Kalimantis!' Jess accused him.

'I am.' He pushed her down into a chair and sat opposite her. 'I assure you that Andros Kalimantis is my name. And now I think it's time you stopped play-acting.' He looked at her warily. 'I think it's time you came clean and told me exactly what kind of game you're playing.'

'What's going on, Jess?' Kitty's childish lips trembled. 'I don't understand what's going on.'

'That makes two of us,' said Jess wryly.

'*Three!*' said the man calling himself Andros. 'Although I suspect there's a simple explanation. It's plain somebody has been using my name.'

Jess said, 'That's a bit far-fetched, isn't it?' but he ignored her.

'Do you have a photograph of your friend?' he asked Kitty.

'No.' She shook her head. 'He said he'd send me one, but ... he never did.'

'For good reason, since he wasn't who he said he was,' observed Jess.

The real Andros ... for that was how she was beginning to think of him ... pulled a wallet out of his shirt pocket. The expensive leather contrasted oddly with his ragged clothes. Flicking through the contents, he produced a photograph and handed it to Kitty.

'Is this him?'

She studied it for a moment. 'Yes,' she whispered. 'That man on the right...that's Andros.' She handed the picture back.

'That's my cousin George,' Andros said. 'Taken last summer when I visited the family in Athens.'

'George?' said Kitty, *'George!* Oh!'

'George Kalimantis,' Andros confirmed. He fixed Jess with a piercing look from eyes as dark and hard as basalt. 'Part of the Kalimantis family, but not such a good mark as *Andros* Kalimantis.'

'I don't know what you mean by "mark",' said Jess. She had a horrible feeling she sounded guilty, but he was looking at her so accusingly that it was hard to sound otherwise.

'I do think you do,' said Andros. 'My family may not be multi-millionaires, but we're certainly worth blackmailing. You messed it up by getting the wrong man.'

'Blackmailing!' Jess heard herself screech. 'Are you out of your mind?'

'It wouldn't be the first time,' he said bitterly.

'Now, look here,' said Jess, recovering her sense of balance and going in to the attack, 'before you hurl any more insults at us, let me inform you that *Kitty* is the injured party in this affair. She's obviously been lied to and generally made a fool of. She trusted this—George— or whatever his name is, and now...' She appealed to her cousin. 'May I tell him, Kitty?'

'Yes,' Kitty whispered. She gave a choked sob and buried her face in her hands.

'Now she's going to have a baby, and I'm here with her to see she gets some kind of support, moral or otherwise. I don't see why *George,*' she pronounced the name venomously, 'should get off scot-free.' She fished in her bag for a hankie and handed it to the weeping girl. 'Don't cry, Kitty, love. These people aren't worth it!'

'Don't overdo it,' Andros said unpleasantly. 'You'll find I'm quite unmoved by easy tears.'

At this, Kitty cried harder than ever, and Jess turned on him like a wildcat. 'You . . . you *bastard*!' she hissed. 'Kitty has every reason to cry. If you had a scrap of decency, you'd be trying to help us find out why this cousin of yours used your name in the first place, instead of making Kitty more upset than ever.'

He gave her the ghost of a smile. 'You fight like a native of the Mani,' he said. 'I assure you I'm as anxious to get to the bottom of this business as you are.' He turned to Kitty. 'I'm sorry if I upset you. Don't cry any more; nothing will be gained by crying.' He said something to the hostess of the taverna who had been standing, goggle-eyed, in the doorway, and when she bustled away he went on, 'I've ordered some coffee to help us recover our tempers.'

Jess ignored this olive branch. 'Does your cousin often go around using your name?' she asked.

'Not to my knowledge. And, believe me,' his face grew harsh, 'he'd better have a good explanation.'

'Well, where can we find him?' asked Jess. 'Or does he keep that a secret, too?'

'George runs our Greek operation. He lives with his mother in Athens,' Andros told her. '*I* live in London.'

'And what do *you* run?' Jess asked, more aggressively than she intended, but she was tired and hungry. I could be sailing right now, she thought resentfully, being chatted up by that nice man from the Brighton Yacht Club, and her stomach growled as if in sympathy.

'I own the company,' Andros said coolly. 'The head office is in London, that's where I'm based. I thought you knew about the Kalimantis Trading Company.'

Jess curled her lip derisively. 'Forgive my ignorance,' she said, 'but the name of Kalimantis doesn't immediately spring to mind when I'm thinking of wealthy people to blackmail. Besides,' her eyes travelled over him scornfully, 'you don't exactly look the part.'

He shrugged his wide shoulders. 'I come to relax in the Mani,' he said. 'I leave my peacock trappings back in the city.' The old woman brought out a tray with three small cups of Greek coffee, three glasses of water, and a dish full of strange-looking flat seeds.

Kitty eyed them suspiciously. 'What on earth are those?' she said when Jess took a handful and munched experimentally.

'I don't know,' said Jess, with her mouth full, 'but they taste good.'

'They're roasted lupin seeds,' Andros informed them, taking some himself. He had beautiful white teeth, Jess noticed.

'I don't know how you can eat those things,' Kitty remarked.

Jess popped a few more into her mouth. 'I happen to be starving,' she said shortly.

'About this baby,' Andros said, 'I've only your word that your cousin's pregnant. I take it she's seen a doctor and has a certificate?'

'I've seen a doctor,' Kitty faltered, 'but...'

'No certificate?' He put a lupin seed into his mouth and chewed it thoughtfully. 'I see. We're supposed to take this fact on trust, are we?'

'Oh, for heaven's sake!' Jess blurted out; she could have kicked herself for not thinking of this. 'Kitty is quite willing to see her doctor again and get you a certificate, aren't you, Kitty?' she asked, and Kitty nodded silently.

'Willing or not, we shall insist on it,' he informed them, getting up from the table. 'And now I'll try and get through to Athens on the taverna phone...'

'Get through to Athens?' Kitty asked blankly.

'In order to arrange a meeting with George and the family tomorrow,' he said coldly. 'The sooner this business is cleared up, the better.'

'He's a horrid man, isn't he?' Kitty whispered as his broad back disappeared.

'*Horrid!*' Jess agreed. 'I just hope the rest of the family isn't like him.'

'I never thought of Andr—I mean, George, having a family,' Kitty said and Jess bit her tongue. No point in saying that Kitty hadn't done any thinking at all as far as Jess could see. Gloomily, she nibbled on lupin seeds, and by the time the dish was empty Andros had joined them again.

'George is out, but I spoke with his mother and you are to meet the family tomorrow,' he told the girls.

'We must find out about buses,' Jess said faintly. This journey was becoming a marathon; God knew when she would be back home at this rate.

Andros brushed this aside. 'I shall drive you,' he said. 'Where are you staying?'

Jess looked at him blankly. 'Wh . . . what?'

'Your hotel?' he said impatiently. 'What hotel are you staying at in Yerolimin?' and when she told him that they hadn't booked into any hotel he gave an exclamation of annoyance and stumped back to use the phone again.

Jess pulled a face. 'You still want to marry into this family?'

Kitty merely blinked and said, 'It'll be all right once I've seen . . . er . . . George again, I *know* it will.'

Andros came back. 'I've booked you a room at the Hotel Aphrodite,' he informed them. 'The taxi's on its way.'

Jess glowered at him. She didn't like being taken over like this. 'How do you know we won't do a bunk?' she said. 'Get the taxi to take us to Athens?'

He smiled grimly. 'In Nikki's taxi? You must be joking. It can barely make it from Yerolimin to Vathia.'

Jess's firm little chin jutted stubbornly. 'We could take a bus.'

'There are no buses until ten tomorrow morning, and I plan to be away long before that.' He looked imperiously down on the two girls. 'I'll pick you up at eight sharp, and be ready. I'm never late!'

With this autocratic command still ringing in her mind, Jess made sure they were waiting on the steps of the hotel by ten to eight the following morning. In spite of a shower and a change of clothes she was stilling feeling the worse for wear. The Hotel Aphrodite was a pleasant little hotel, but Kitty had complained constantly from the moment they had arrived. They had eaten at a taverna on the quayside, where she'd picked at her food, and sent things back, and generally been a pain in the neck. When they'd returned to their modest room she'd bitched because the bathroom was down the corridor, and then she'd discovered that there was no hot-water tap over the little washbasin, and she'd started on about that. Jess had been ready to brain her with a coat hanger! This morning Kitty had demonstrated that she did indeed suffer from morning sickness, and had woken Jess early to prove it! If his Lordship Kalimantis had been holding Kitty's head this morning, he wouldn't keep nattering on about doctors' certificates, Jess thought rancorously as he drew up in his rented Mercedes on the dot of eight.

This morning he looked less like the local tramp and more the successful businessman. He wore a gray silk suit, with a silk tie striped in shades of trendy pink. His hair had been sleeked back off his forehead into smooth raven waves, and he was wearing expensive-looking leather shoes.

But this finery didn't disguise the powerful shoulders or the physical strength of the man. He still looks like a thug to me, Jess thought sourly. He might be as rich as Croesus, but he's still a pirate!

'I can sit in the back with Kitty,' she said when he held the front passenger door open for her.

'Don't be silly, she'll be much too cramped.' He pushed her firmly into the front seat. 'Miss Taylor looks a bit under the weather. This way she can lie down on the back seat if she wants to.'

He drove fast and competently, and the journey out of the Mani was much faster than the one into it, but it still took them six hours. They stopped for lunch at a taverna outside Sparta and ate salad that was generously dotted with ripe black olives, spicy feta cheese and wedges of plump tomatoes. This was accompanied by a dish of fried eggs, thick slices of country bread, and glasses of iced coffee. Jess was hungry after their light breakfast, and even Kitty seemed to have recovered her appetite and tucked in without her usual complaints. The meal was slightly marred when Jess and Andros became involved in an argument because she insisted on paying for their lunch.

He raised his black brows. 'You'll never become rich that way. But if you insist...'

'I do!' She did some quick mental arithmetic and plunked some drachmas down on the table. 'There! That's our share.' Her generous mouth grew firm. 'One is rich when one is not beholden,' she said, adding silently, and beholden to you is something I don't intend to be.

Kitty gave a great sigh and, waving her paper serviette in front of her face like a fan, asked, 'Could we get moving, do you think? It's cooler in the car, with the windows down.' And so they set off again along the road that seemed to tremble in the shimmering heat.

They arrived in Athens while the city was still wrapped in the siesta. Not that Athens ever really seems to rest. Even though the shops and offices close during the heat of the day the tourists still throng the streets and sit gasping at café tables on Syntagma square; sipping cold drinks, maps grasped in sweaty palms, clothes clinging stickily.

The Kalimantis family home turned out to be a handsome four-storey building with a fine view of the Acropolis. The street was shady with plane trees, quiet, and obviously expensive. Anything with a view like that would be, thought Jess.

'I spoke to George on the phone this morning, and we thought it would be better if we met with him privately first,' said Andros. He murmured a greeting to a white-jacketed servant who opened the heavy doors for them.

Jess was aware of a great deal of marble and old wood which gleamed like light on water. Vases of flowers were reflected in antique mirrors, curtains of ivory silk hung at the windows, but she was too keyed-up at the thought of the coming confrontation with George Kalimantis to take much in.

'George will be waiting for us in the study,' Andros said, 'but first, perhaps you'd like to have a wash after the journey.' He summoned a maid who led them to a downstairs cloakroom which sparkled with gold-plated taps and a quantity of mirrors.

While she dried her face on a fluffy apricot-coloured towel, Jess asked, 'Did you know that George was rich? You never mentioned it.'

'I never thought about it,' answered Kitty, rubbing blusher into her pale cheeks. 'I mean...we went to super places for dinner and stuff like that, but so what? He was in London on business, and I just took it for granted that he'd have money to spend. Expense accounts...you know, that sort of thing.' She sighed reminiscently.

'This is a bit more than expense-account cash,' Jess murmured, looking at the cream marble and array of perfume bottles. 'It looks as if "Awful Andros" wasn't exaggerating when he said the family had money.'

'I don't want their money.' Kitty's lips trembled. 'I just want George to marry me.'

Jess loosened her hair from its French braid, pulling her fingers through the silky mass. '*Please,* Kitty,' she said urgently, 'please don't set your heart on marriage. This George doesn't sound like the marrying type to me...'

Kitty stuck out her bottom lip. 'But I *want* to marry him,' she insisted. 'I'm going to have his baby.'

'I don't want to preach to you, Kit-Kat,' said Jess, 'but we've both had vivid examples of how easy it is for a marriage to go wrong. I mean...' She searched for the right words. 'I mean... what with *my* mother's three marriages, and Auntie Mary's...er...track record...'

'I don't believe Mummy was ever really in love with any of those men,' Kitty said stoutly, and Jess, remembering the succession of 'uncles' that had drifted through Kitty's life, was inclined to agree. But she persisted, for she was convinced her cousin was hurtling towards disaster.

'Your mother *thought* she was in love though, didn't she, Kitty? Remember how she used to...' She was going to say 'go on about it', but decided to amend that to 'talk about it'.

'It wasn't the same,' Kitty whimpered. 'I know it wasn't.'

'Well, OK!' sighed Jess. 'If you *must* marry him...and if he's willing...so be it! But, if he's *not* willing, I think the first thing we must do when we get home is find you a good solicitor.'

'*Stop it,* Jess!' cried Kitty, her eyes filling with tears.

'I just want you to be prepared, Kitty. You haven't got a penny in the world, and I don't make enough to support you. It's only right George Kalimantis should help.' She looked around the resplendent bathroom. 'He can certainly afford it.'

'Stop *talking* like that,' demanded her cousin. 'I tell you he loves me. He won't let me down.'

Deciding that it was useless to point out that men who were seriously in love didn't usually lie about their names, disappear, and then return all your letters unopened, Jess picked up her brush and vigorously dealt with her unpinned hair. 'We'd better get a move on or they'll think we're lost,' was all she said as her glossy mane crackled under the brush.

'Do I look all right?' asked Kitty anxiously.

'You look terrific, kiddo,' Jess assured her as Kitty hopelessly pulled at the wrinkled skirt of her green cotton dress. 'A credit to us both.'

She scooped up her hairpins and dropped them into her make-up purse. Her head hurt from hours of wearing her hair braided, so she had left it loose, a dark gold frame for her lovely face. She was pleased to see that her cotton-knit skirt and matching top were pristine and uncrushed. The delphinium-blue colour seemed to add sheen to her hair and radiant complexion.

Andros was waiting for them. His eyes, black as pitch, rested for a moment on Jess, who glowed like a beautiful warm candle, reducing Kitty's prettiness to a dim gleam. Then, 'This way,' he said, leading them down the hall.

'In here.' He opened the door of a book-lined study. A large, leather-topped desk stood at one end, flanked by two armchairs. Kitty gave a little cry as a young man got up from one of them.

She had been right, Jess thought, George Kalimantis was certainly very handsome. He was not as tall as his cousin, and he was slight. But he *was* stunningly good-looking, with a profile that could have been cut on a Greek coin. He was young, in his early twenties, Jess judged, and his immaturity was heightened by his expression, which at the moment was sulky, like a little boy caught stealing jam.

Kitty started to turn towards him, but stopped when he made no move to meet her, and Jess felt a stab of sympathy for the girl.

There was an awkward silence, then George Kalimantis said, 'Hello, Kitty. How are you?' His English, unlike Andros's, was heavily accented.

'All...all right!' Kitty replied. Her face was tragic.

'I don't think you've met Kitty's cousin, Jessica Firbank, have you, George?' said Andros.

Jess glared at George as he mumbled a greeting. 'If I *had* met him, I don't suppose he would have given me his real name,' she said cuttingly.

George flushed a dull red. 'That was foolish,' he said, 'but it was done from...from...'

Andros cut in, 'From vanity. Apparently George doesn't find his name romantic enough when he's in England, so he uses mine.' His mouth tightened. 'He tells me he finds it makes a better impression on the ladies.'

'It is my name, too,' said George sullenly. 'My full name is George *Andros* Kalimantis.'

'Which you never use, except on legal documents,' said Andros. He indicated the chairs. 'Why don't we sit down? This discussion is liable to take some time, we might as well be comfortable.'

Kitty gave a muffled sob and collapsed into the nearest chair, and George said gruffly, 'Do not cry, Kitty. *Please!*'

'I ca...can't help it,' she sobbed. 'I thought you loved me.' And George, passing his hand over his immaculate hair, looked shifty.

Jess came up to Kitty and, taking her cousin's limp little hand, said softly, 'Don't cry, Kit-Kat...you'll just make yourself ill, and you'll ruin your looks.' A psychological ploy that worked, for after a few moments Kitty mopped her eyes and pulled herself together.

'Would you like a glass of water, Miss Taylor?' Andros asked.

'No, th-thank you,' Kitty hiccuped, 'I'm all right now.'

George sat himself in the chair across from Kitty's. 'Andros tells me there is to be a child. Is this true?' he said. His face was a mask of despair, but there was an air of theatricality about George Kalimantis that Jess found offensive.

'I'm two months pregnant,' Kitty whispered, so softly she was barely audible. 'I found out after you'd gone...I wrote you about it.'

He turned red and when Jess said tersely, 'You sent her letters back unopened,' he turned a deeper shade.

'So...' he said at last, 'you are to bear my child?' Kitty nodded dumbly. 'So...' He lifted his hands in a gesture of hopelessness and said, 'What choice do I have? I must do the honourable thing and give my child a name.'

Kitty's head jerked up and at the same moment Jess said, 'We didn't come here begging for marriage.'

'*Jess!*' Kitty hissed.

Andros asked, 'Why *did* you come here, then?'

'To make sure that Kitty got a fair deal. She can't afford to bring up a child alone.'

'I wondered how long it would be before we got on to the subject of money,' Andros said, linking his strong brown hands and leaning them on the desk.

Jess felt her temper fraying. She snapped, 'I don't know the law in this country, but in England the father is expected to contribute towards the welfare of the child. We shall go to court if necessary.'

George leapt to his feet. 'There is no need for this kind of talk,' he said dramatically. 'I have offered to do the honorable thing. What more do you want from me?'

'I'm sure Kitty doesn't want you to *sacrifice* yourself,' said Jess, 'and you're making it quite plain that that's what it would be.'

Kitty suddenly seemed to find her courage, and she fairly shouted at Jess, 'Do be quiet! Of *course* I want to marry him.'

'Why?' replied Jess, stung. 'He obviously doesn't want to marry *you*!'

Andros took charge. 'I take it you're not in favour of a shot-gun wedding,' he said to Jess.

'No, I'm not,' agreed Jess. 'I think shot-guns belong in wars, not weddings.'

'I agree with you,' said Andros, 'which leaves us with the question of a settlement.'

'But I *want* to marry Andros...I mean, George,' Kitty cried. 'I love him!'

George came to Jess and said angrily, 'There will be no question of guns. It is unthinkable for the son of a Kalimantis to grow up illegitimate. It is my *duty* to give him my name.'

'What if he's a girl?' asked Jess with deceptive sweetness.

Kitty pleaded, 'Jess, *please*! George is willing to marry me. That's all that matters.'

'There is the family to consider,' Andros said to his cousin. 'I doubt if your mother will approve of the match.'

'She will have to approve,' said George, throwing back his head dramatically. 'The Kalimantis honour is at stake. I have no choice...Mama must be made to see that.'

Jess felt her hackles rise. 'I don't know your mama,' she said, 'but as a member of Kitty's family I can tell you I'm not over the moon about *you*, and I certainly don't think Kitty should marry you.'

George glared at her. 'That is of no concern to me,' he said. 'You are not Greek and have no Maniot heritage, so you cannot understand...'

Andros surprised her by saying, 'For once I agree with Miss Firbank. I think such a marriage will bring nothing but unhappiness, and in the end it will bring nothing but discredit to the name of Kalimantis.'

So much for *his* support, thought Jess. All the pair of them care about is their wretched family. 'To be perfectly frank,' she said in what she hoped was a tone of scathing contempt, 'I don't care if the whole Kalimantis tribe winds up at the bottom of the Aegean Sea ... but before they do I think certain obligations must be met.'

'I presume you're talking about *financial* obligations,' Andros said, looking at her with mistrust.

George cried out, 'All this is just so much talk! It does not change the fact that there is to be a child. It shall ... *must* ... have my name. I do not care that you are all against me.' He went to Kitty and sank to his knees before her, and Jess had to repress a wild desire to giggle. 'I make a formal proposal to you, Kitty. I am willing to do my duty for the sake of our child. Will you marry me?'

Looking most unhappy, Kitty murmured, 'Yes,' and then, to Jess's relief, George got up and fastidiously brushed the knees of his elegant black trousers.

There was a stiff silence.

'Well, that's that, I suppose!' Jess said.

'Not quite,' said Andros. 'Now we must inform the family. They are waiting upstairs.' He fixed George with an ironic eye. 'It may take a while.' He got up and faced Kitty. 'I trust you won't object to seeing the Kalimantis family doctor, to get the pregnancy confirmed,' he said.

'What's wrong with her own doctor in London?' asked Jess. 'Or are British doctors discounted by *the family*?'

'That would be acceptable,' Andros said. There was an edge to his deep voice. 'As long as he's reputable.'

Jess's patience now gave way and she whirled on him. 'I'm sick and tired of your cheap insults,' she fumed. 'First it's blackmail, and now you seem to think we're in cahoots with a shady doctor.'

'Don't protest too much, Miss Firbank,' Andros said. 'It lessens your credibility.'

She took a deep breath in order to regain her self-control. 'Perhaps it's because I don't come from the same kind of background as you,' she said softly. 'I don't become paranoid every time money's mentioned. Nor do I——' she raised her eyes, which belied her soft voice and were blazing '—nor do I gratuitously insult people who are simply trying to see that justice is done.'

'Justice is one thing,' Andros observed. 'Extortion is something else.'

Jess's voice rose several decibels. 'There you go again!' she screeched.

He remained unruffled. 'Let's just say I'm cautious,' he said. 'I've learnt to be.'

'To misquote you,' Jess bit back, 'caution's one thing—rudeness is another!'

Andros smiled grimly and murmured, '*Touché,* Miss Firbank.'

'We are wasting time,' George said, 'the family is waiting.' He seemed to clench his jaw. 'And Mama,' he added.

Andros gave the ghost of a malicious grin, before rising from the desk and leading the way from the room.

They climbed a wide marble staircase that had balustrades of olive wood carved in an intricate pattern of vines. The walls were hung with portraits. Kalimantis ancestors, Jess supposed. Some of the men certainly resembled Andros, and she shivered a little under their dark painted stares.

They entered an upstairs sitting-room. Here there were rich Persian rugs glowing with colour on the marble floor. From an icon on one wall came the golden gleam of painted haloes. Comfortable armchairs covered in some sort of woven material were scattered around the room, but no one lounged in them. Several black-clad elderly ladies were perched on straight-backed chairs, glaring like a gaggle of bad-tempered geese. This, apparently, was the family.

The meeting with George's mother had all the aspects of a bad foreign film. This lady was small, imperious, and appeared to possess the instincts of a Greek tragedian; and the clash between her and her son was worthy of star billing at the nearby Amphitheatre of Dionysus.

George and Andros were the only members of this gathering who spoke English, so most of the proceedings were lost on Jess, but one didn't need to be a linguist to realise that Mrs Kalimantis was furious at the prospect of acquiring Kitty as a daughter-in-law. She ranted at her son and he ranted back, while the elderly ladies threw in the odd comment like a well rehearsed Greek chorus.

Andros lounged in his chair, seemingly unaffected by all this. 'I take it the family aren't too pleased with the news?' Jess said to him, after a particularly noisy interchange.

'My Aunt Cassandra had already picked out a wife for George,' he explained, 'and this has put a spanner in the works.'

'I can see that it would,' Jess murmured.

Eventually the Greek chorus quieted, Mrs Kalimantis wiped her eyes, and after a venomous glance in the direction of the hapless Kitty addressed herself to Andros.

'What's the problem now?' asked Jess when she'd finished.

'George insists that his mother give him the Kalimantis engagement ring,' Andros replied. His air of amused indolence had deserted him and he seemed cautious again.

'And what is the Kalimantis engagement ring?' Jess enquired.

George answered her. 'It is a ring that has been in our family for many years,' he said. 'It is the tradition that the first Kalimantis man to marry in each generation gives it to his fiancée. My mother refuses to part with it now.' He turned to Andros. 'And in this you support her,' he accused.

'I'm sure Miss Taylor would be satisfied with a more modest ring,' Andros said smoothly.

'*Ochi*. No!' exclaimed George, embarking into a passionate torrent of Greek.

This flood was finally halted when his mother, with a gesture worthy of Medea, tore a ring from her finger and flung it at her son.

'Hah! *Efkharisto*. Thank you, Mama!,' he said histrionically, stooping to pick it up and putting it on Kitty's finger.

'Oh!' said Kitty, staring at the heavy jewel. She held out her hand to Jess, and a large square-cut emerald surrounded by diamonds glittered in the light. 'Look, Jess, isn't it something?'

'Very handsome,' Jess agreed. It was clear why Mrs Kalimantis had been so reluctant. The ring must be worth a fortune!

After all the dramatics, a pall of gloom seemed to settle on the party, even though a bottle of Mantinia, a light wine that comes from the Peloponnese, and a dish of nut cakes were produced. The elderly ladies dabbed at their eyes and glowered at George, and George's mother glowered at her future daughter-in-law.

Jess put aside her wine. She didn't enjoy pretending that this was an occasion for celebration, and she noticed that Andros did the same.

Glancing at her watch, she remarked to Kitty that they should be getting to the airport if they intended catching their plane.

'I trust,' said Andros, 'that you and Miss Taylor are satisfied.' He gave a significant look at the emerald winking on Kitty's finger like green fire.

Two spots of colour appeared in Jess's cheeks, and her gray eyes glittered. 'We came to see that Kitty got a fair deal,' she said, 'and now, since she seems to think she has, there's no reason for me to hang around.' She said to her cousin, 'I have to work tomorrow, Kitty, but you don't have to come with me if you don't want to.'

'Oh, I think I'd better.' She cast an appealing look at George, perhaps hoping that he would ask her to stay, but he didn't.

Andros offered to drive them to the airport. 'George will come, too,' he said. 'He and Miss Taylor can discuss the plans for their wedding in the car.'

George gave him a look of intense misery and, after Kitty had said a half-hearted goodbye to the assembled company, who pointedly ignored her, they left the room.

'When will I see you again, George?' Kitty asked wistfully when they were sitting in the car.

George became evasive. 'I am not sure...there is much for me to do at the office...'

'Couldn't you get over to London next weekend?' she asked. 'Or I could come to you.'

'We will see, Kitty...we will see.' His voice grew petulant. 'Do not nag me, please.'

What a *weed* he is! Jess thought contemptuously. What can Kitty be thinking of, to tie herself to a man like that? She stole a glance from under her thick lashes at Andros's face. His chin jutted squarely, he looked as if he was carved from stone. She found it difficult to imagine that he and George were related. I bet Andros wouldn't behave like that, she thought. He's got more character, and she thought regretfully that it was a pity they had not met under different circumstances, because in spite of everything she had to admit that she found his company exhilarating. There was a kind of energy that flowed between them. When they had first met, she'd known he fancied her, and for her part she had never met a man quite like him before. It would have been fun to get to know him better, she thought wistfully. Ah, well... She spent the rest of the journey looking out of the car at the countless shop windows that were filled with lighting fixtures, trying not to dwell on what might have been.

At the airport, it became clear that George couldn't wait to leave. 'I do not enjoy long farewells,' he said, giving his fiancée a peck on the cheek. '*Kali nikhta,* Miss Firbank. Kitty, I shall phone you.' He moved hastily towards the exit.

'Goodbye, Mr Kalimantis,' said Jess to his departing back. She started to propel Kitty towards the departure lounge, but Andros laid a restraining hand on her arm.

'A word with you,' he said, leading her out of Kitty's earshot.

He leaned over her. He was so close, she could see the shadow of his beard, and she found herself wondering if he had to shave more than once a day. 'You and Miss Taylor seem plausible enough,' he said, 'but I'm still not convinced. I think you should know that I intend to have you both investigated.'

This took her breath away, but she managed to say calmly, 'Go ahead, it's your privilege. You could also wait seven months for the irrefutable proof, of course.' She gave a humourless smile which he didn't return.

'George has Miss Taylor's address. If you'll just give me yours.' He handed her a gilt-edged notebook and gold pen, and with fingers that shook from anger she scribbled down the address of The Saracen's Head.

He glanced down at what she'd written. 'You live in a hotel?'

'It's where I work,' she said coldly. 'I'm a barmaid there.'

'Perhaps I'll drop in for a drink some time,' he said. 'Check it out.'

'You don't need to drop in for a drink to do that. Just get in touch with my boss. He'll tell you all you want to know.'

She turned to leave, but again he caught her by the arm and held her fast.

'I think it only fair to warn you that I've had some...' He hesitated. 'Some experience with blackmail.'

'I really don't care to know about your sordid past,' she said haughtily, thinking it would take a brave person to blackmail a tough character like him.

'I'm simply warning you,' he said quietly. 'You're not dealing with an innocent. You'd be advised to watch your step.'

Exasperated, she pulled herself out of his grasp. 'I don't have to watch anything,' she said. 'Kitty and I have nothing to hide.'

As she walked to where Kitty was waiting she heard him murmur, 'I hope so,' but she didn't turn back. Not until she'd gone through the barrier, and then she found that his dark eyes were still fixed unwaveringly on her. With a disdainful shrug, she turned her back on him again, and went into the departure lounge.

CHAPTER THREE

JESS was thankful to be back home. Of the many bed-sitters she'd inhabited over the years, her upper-floor room in the Talbots' rambling house in Hove was her favourite. It was big and airy, and if she stood on a chair she could glimpse a wedge of blue sea between the chimney-pots. She had made cretonne cushions for the sofa, hung plants at the windows, and bought some bits and pieces from antique shops in the famous Brighton 'Lanes'. A Victorian cup and saucer, a china cat, and—her most extravagant purchase—a miniature brass carriage clock that had taken a full month's salary.

Her landlady was still up, watching a late-night movie on television, when Jess let herself in to the hall.

'You're back then, lovey, are you?' said Mrs Talbot, poking her face round the door. 'Dad! Jess is back,' she said over her shoulder to her husband. 'I was just going to make a cup of cocoa for Dad and myself,' she said. 'Come on in and have a cup with us.'

Jess didn't really want cocoa, all she wanted was bed, but she didn't have the energy to refuse, having experienced Mrs Talbot's persistence in the past, so she accepted and went into the kitchen with her landlady to help.

Mrs Talbot looked at her critically. 'You're not a bit tanned,' she said. 'Didn't you have good weather?'

'It was lovely,' said Jess, putting the bottle of milk back in the fridge, 'but this wasn't a holiday, so I didn't get any time to loll about in the sun.'

'Business, was it?' Mrs Talbot probed; she liked to know what was going on. 'Just reach up and fetch me

43

that big plate—the one with the roses on it, will you, Jess?'

'Family business,' Jess said vaguely.

'I didn't know you had any family in Greece,' said Mrs Talbot, putting biscuits on to the plate Jess had handed her.

'Very distant family,' said Jess, realising that this was true, for she *would* be distantly related to the Kalimantis family after the wedding. She might meet Andros sometimes over the years, at widely spaced family gatherings. She wondered if there would always be that current of attraction between them. That unspoken excitement.

'Come back, Jess!' Mrs Talbot teased. 'You're miles away. Still in Greece, were you?'

'No, just suffering from jet-lag.'

'Dreaming about some nice boy, more like it,' Mrs Talbot chuckled. 'You looked regularly moon-struck.'

'I didn't meet anybody,' Jess protested, 'at least, nobody interesting.'

But Mrs Talbot smiled and said, 'Don't tell me! Why look at you! You're blushing. Well, good luck to you, I say. You enjoy yourself while you're young.'

'I'll try!' said Jess, taking the tray and leading the way to the front room.

Apart from telling her saturnine husband, 'Looks like our Jess met someone nice in Greece,' her landlady kept off the subject, but Jess was surprised at herself. She'd never been the sort who blushed easily, and now here she was, colouring just because she'd been caught *thinking* about Andros. It was just as well she wouldn't be seeing much of him, at this rate. Not if she was going to behave like that!

But by the following morning, Greece, Andros, and the village of towers seemed miles away. It was drizzling in Brighton, the sea was as grey as Jess's eyes, and the holidaymakers were bundled up against the chill wind that whipped through the streets, making people think of warm soup and fires, instead of cool drinks and swimming.

Because of the weather, The Saracen's Head was busier than usual. Her boss's wife, Ann, who did the lunches, had made chilli, and Jess was rushed off her feet, serving bowls of the spicy bean stew. She was glad to be working again, even if she was still tired and her job was rather boring, for the activity took her mind off Kitty and, since that topic seemed to steer her thoughts to Andros, to be busy was a blessing.

When the pub had closed after lunch, Jess offered to help Ann in the kitchen. They were short-staffed at the moment, one of the two women who helped out with the washing up was away on her annual holiday, so Jess tied on an apron and started scrubbing at the empty pots. She had just finished the last one, and was putting on the kettle for coffee when Ted Purvis came in. 'Still at it, girls?' he said, putting an arm round his wife's waist. He nodded in Jess's direction. 'That's what I call dedicated help!'

'She won't be dedicated much longer, you great lummox,' said Ann, giving him a gentle push. 'Not unless she gets a reviving cup of coffee. Why don't you get the mugs out? Lend a hand instead of always supervising.'

'I will. Don't nag me,' he grinned, giving Ann a friendly pat on her behind on his way to the cupboard.

Ann smiled fondly. She and Ted had married several years ago, but they still appeared to be happy. To Jess, their devotion was a constant, and delightful, surprise. She only hoped it would last!

'I had a phone call about you just now, Jess,' Ted said as he spooned instant coffee into three mugs.

'Really?' She removed the big butcher's apron. 'What about?'

'Oh, just general enquiries: wanting to know how long you'd worked for us, where you'd worked before. That sort of thing.'

Jess poured hot water over the coffee. She guessed instantly that Andros had made good his threat to have her investigated. Well, he certainly hadn't wasted much time! Putting the kettle back on the stove, she asked casually, 'Who was making the enquiries?'

'I dunno! I assumed it was a credit rating,' Ted told her, spooning sugar into his coffee. 'I thought maybe you'd applied for a student loan. You did mention that you wanted to go to university. For what it's worth, I told them you were a gem. Told them you make the best cup of instant coffee in Sussex!' They laughed, and the matter was forgotten.

At least, the Purvises forgot it. Jess didn't. Walking home along the front later that day, the rain misting her thick blonde hair, she seethed with indignation. Oh, she didn't blame him for checking up. Common sense told her that the Kalimantis clan would have to be cautious. But to do it so dispassionately! She could have given him the information he wanted, but by using a firm of professional investigators he had as good as told her he considered her a liar.

She kicked at a pebble lying on the path in front of her. How she wished she'd never agreed to go with Kitty in the first place, then she would never have met this big dark man. This man whose personality was so overpowering that she didn't seem able to get him out of her mind. She picked up the pebble and hurled it back on to the beach. She would work on forgetting the lot of them. She'd go out and play—extra hard! Banish all thoughts of Andros Kalimantis from her life!

During the next two weeks, the weather cleared and grew warm again. The man with the sailboat reappeared and took Jess out sailing; they went dancing in the evenings, or joined friends for drinks or the theatre. Her life was pleasant and the memory of Andros began to fade, but it never went totally away. All the time, tucked away in the back of her mind was the memory of a big man who looked like a pirate, with a voice that would have melted granite, and in spite of herself this memory made her real-life admirers seem insipid.

During this time she didn't see Kitty, but they spoke on the phone occasionally and Jess gathered that George had not come to London, nor had Kitty visited Athens. On her last call, Kitty mentioned that she had received a letter from her old boyfriend. 'He's pleased to be back in Australia,' she'd said, 'he really likes it.' She sounded wistful, but nothing more had been said on the subject.

The following Saturday night, Jess was working in the bar. Tony, her sailing friend, was there nursing a pint of lager, for they planned to go for a meal when she finished work. The pub was busy, but not frantic, so Jess had time to chat with some of the 'regulars' while she served. She was just about to hand a foaming pint of ale to a customer when Andros, tall and unmistakable, came in. The laugh died in her throat and she nearly spilled the drink.

His jet-black eyes fixed themselves on her, but he didn't come over at first; he simply stood looking at her, his face as hard as iron.

Her heart started to pump, but she stretched her mouth into a smile and said in her best professional manner, 'Yes, sir, what can I do for you?'

He reached the bar in two strides and said, with a repressed anger that made her secretly quail, 'You can come out from behind that bloody bar. I want to talk to you.'

'I'm afraid I can't do that,' she said, turning away and rinsing glasses at the bar-sink, 'I'm not free to socialise until closing time.'

'What I have to say hardly comes under the heading of socialising,' he snarled, and she saw that under his tan his face was white.

His anger was catching and she snapped back, 'Whatever it is, it'll have to wait until I've finished work.

Which will be in...' she pushed back the cuff of her purple cotton jump suit to look at her watch '...in half an hour.'

He drew an impatient breath. 'Very well. I'll have a brandy and soda, and I'll wait for you,' he jerked his head in the direction of one of the small tables against the wall, 'over there. And don't try a disappearing act through the back door.'

'I don't know what you're talking about,' she said as she poured his brandy. 'I think you must be raving mad.'

He put some money down on the bar to pay for his drink. 'You're a very good actress,' he said, 'but you can take off your make-up, the play's over.'

'Is this man bothering you, Jess?' asked Tony.

'It's all right,' she said hastily, going to the till for Andros's change. Tony was a fair-sized man, but compared to Andros he was puny. The thought of them getting into any kind of scrap was ludicrous, Andros could have tossed him out of the pub with one hand tied behind him. 'Andros is ... er ... a friend from Greece,' she said.

'He doesn't sound very Greek to me,' Tony said, and Jess thought he didn't sound very friendly either, but in an attempt to smooth things over she said, 'I suppose technically you're not really a Greek, are you?'

Andros ignored this. 'I'll wait till you're through here,' he said, and nodding dourly at Tony he picked up his brandy, and went over to his table.

She arranged with the reluctant Tony to meet him later on at the restaurant. 'What is this fellow to you, anyway?' he grumbled.

'*Nothing!* Believe me, nothing at all!' she reassured him, then she hurried to collect some dirty glasses and clean off some tables, for Ted was beginning to look put out at what might have seemed like an idle flirtation on company time.

When the last customer had left she went to the little cloakroom. She looked critically in the mirror. Her jumpsuit was new, and showed off her curves to advantage. She'd piled her toffee-coloured hair up into a topknot this evening, and this style showed off her graceful neck and delicate ears. Carefully, she added some mascara to her thick lashes and applied lip-gloss. She was looking good tonight! Not that it would make a jot of difference to Andros whether she was looking nice or not, but it was good for her morale. Looking her best was like wearing armour—and she needed something to protect herself from Andros's anger.

Poking her head through the kitchen door she asked, 'OK if I leave now?'

'Sure, Jess,' said Ann, emptying a dish of pickled onions into a jar. 'Your new boyfriend is still waiting for you in the bar.'

'He's *not* a boyfriend,' Jess said firmly. Ann raised an eyebrow. 'Just...er...family.'

'Some family,' laughed Ann. 'He's got a face like a thundercloud.'

Jess attempted to make light of it. 'Don't be fooled, actually he's a pussy-cat.'

'Well, I hope his claws are clipped,' said Ann, and Jess smiled weakly.

Andros was standing by the door. All but one light in the bar had been extinguished, and his shadow loomed eerily. Jess felt ridiculously nervous as she walked towards him, her heels clacking loudly on the hard floor. 'I hope this won't take long,' she said, 'my date's waiting.'

He remarked grimly, 'You have more serious things to worry about than a broken date.'

Quickly, she replied, 'I've no intention of breaking it.'

'We'll see.' His jaw set. 'You may not feel like celebrating when I'm finished with you.'

'I haven't the remotest idea what you're talking about,' she said, aware that he was scarcely bothering to listen to her.

'Cut it out, Miss Firbank!' He opened the door to the street. 'I presume you don't want your employers to hear what you've been up to. Shall we take a walk?' He took her arm above the elbow, and his grip was not gentle. They started walking down towards the sea. She stole a sidelong glance at him. He was wearing a black shirt and trousers under a grey linen jacket, which made him look to Jess like a prison-warder, and she had the uncomfortable feeling that she was indeed his prisoner.

There were not many people walking along the front. Muted sounds of music from the big hotels that faced the beach drifted and mingled with the whisper of the surf as it swept over the stones, tumbling them back and forth on the shore. Usually she found this a peaceful sound, but tonight, with Andros striding beside her, his hand digging into the flesh of her upper arm, it sounded more like the hissing of a malevolent animal about to attack.

He halted close to one of the streetlights and swung her round to face him. Her hair was gilded by the light, a silky mop of dark gold.

'It was a very neat trick you and your cousin pulled off,' he said, releasing her arm at last, 'and if it wasn't for me you would have got away with it—George was so thankful to be free!'

She made a great play of rubbing her arm. 'I honestly don't know what you're talking about,' she said. 'I think you must be mad.'

'Come now, Jess—I presume at this stage of our relationship I may call you that?' he asked with ironic courtesy. 'Come now, the jig's up! I'm pretty sure you masterminded the whole thing, so you might as well own up without all this play-acting.'

'You exasperating, pig-headed, bloody awful *man*!' she exploded, hammering at his chest with her fists, which was as ineffectual as beating against an iron door with a handful of twigs.

He grasped both her hands in one of his and held them firmly. 'You don't know about the letter, or that Kitty's gone, I suppose.'

'*Gone?*' She looked up at him, her beautiful eyes wide. 'What do you mean...*gone*?'

'Well, since you insist on playing this charade...' He let go of her hands and reached into the pocket of his jacket. 'Yesterday, George received this letter.' He passed a white envelope to Jess, and she recognised Kitty's childish hand.

Cautiously, as if it might bite, she drew the letter out and held the single sheet of paper to the light. 'Oh, lord!' she said when she'd read it.

The letter explained that Kitty had suffered a miscarriage, so there was no longer any need for George to marry her. Well, not marrying George was OK, thought Jess. That was cause for rejoicing, in fact. It was what followed that made her go cold.

'I've decided that I want to start a new life in Australia,' Kitty had written, 'so I had to pawn your ring to get money for my fare. I am enclosing the pawn ticket, and I will pay you back as soon as I get settled. Please don't think badly of me. Kitty.'

'Oh, lord!' said Jess again, handing back the letter.

'What's wrong?' he asked. 'Wasn't she supposed to disappear? Has your accomplice double-crossed you?'

'I do wish you'd stop talking like a bad detective novel!' Jess snapped. 'She's not my accomplice.'

'No? What about the clever idea of pawning a valuable ring? That way you acquire a tidy sum of money without the dangerous business of blackmailing the victim.'

'You seem to have a fixation about blackmail,' Jess said wearily.

'I have good cause,' Andros retorted.

'All I wanted was for Kitty to get some financial help when the baby came.'

'*What baby?*' he said harshly. 'I'm beginning to think that was just a hoax to frighten George.'

'A hoax!' Her voice rose to an undignified squeak. 'I tell you she had morning sickness!'

'*You* tell me—yes! You've told me a lot, Jessica Firbank, but you've never given me any *proof.* I'm just supposed to take your word for everything, is that it? Meanwhile your cousin . . . or accomplice . . . or whatever she is, makes off with a valuable ring, leaving me with nothing but a *pawn ticket.*' His eyes glittered like black glass.

Jess leant against the lamp-post for support. 'Did . . . didn't Kitty send you a doctor's certificate?'

'Of course she didn't!' he said contemptuously.

Dear God, Jess thought wildly, when I see Kitty again I'll *strangle* her. Then her brain started to function. 'Her doctor!' she cried, 'All you have to do is go to her doctor.'

'Where do I find him?'

Her face fell. 'I don't know. But her flatmates might. We could ask them.'

He glared at her. 'And just how do we do that?'

'*Phone* them, of course!' She saw a phone box a few yards further on and started towards it, searching in her purse for change as she went.

'I'll do the talking when we get through,' he said, coming up to her. 'I don't want any more second-hand messages from you.'

Jess dialled the number and then handed him the receiver. 'Be my guest,' she said coldly.

He didn't take it. 'You can introduce me. Just say I'm a friend who's anxious to get in touch with Miss Taylor.'

A British phone box isn't the most spacious place in the world, and with Andros squeezed in with her it assumed the proportions of a small sentry box. She was crushed against him, and when finally one of Kitty's flat-mates answered he hooked his arm round Jess's neck so that she could share the receiver with him. She could feel his warm breath on her cheek, see the trimmed black hairs of his moustache. I wonder what that would feel like if he kissed me, she thought, and she coloured in the darkness.

The girls didn't know the name of Kitty's doctor, but they did confirm the fact that Kitty had been pregnant, and that she had lost the baby some days ago. She had left for Australia as soon as she'd recovered from the miscarriage.

'Much too soon,' her flatmate said, 'but you know what Kitty is!'

'Well, if you would let me know where I can get in touch with Miss Taylor as soon as you know yourself, I'd appreciate it,' said Andros into the phone, and after he'd given his London address he hung up.

When they came out of the stuffy phone box, he turned to Jess. 'Well, you were telling the truth about the pregnancy at any rate,' he said.

Wonderful! Jess muttered to herself. A really handsome apology!

'However,' he went on, 'we still don't know her address in Australia. If indeed she's there.'

'Oh yes, I'm sure she is,' she said positively. 'She's gone back to Charlie.'

He stopped in his tracks. 'And who is *Charlie*? Another of your associates?'

She ran her fingers through her hair, loosening several glossy strands in the process. 'Oh, lord! Are you starting that again? Charlie is her old boyfriend. He went back to Australia a couple of months ago.'

'And Kitty needed money to join him?' His mouth twisted ironically. 'What a complicated way to get it.'

'Are you suggesting Kitty got herself pregnant in order to get an engagement ring, then managed to lose the baby in order to *sell* it?' Her voice was as sharp as the point of a needle.

They stood together by the railing, looking out at the gently swaying sea. The Palace pier stretched out from the shore like a dark centipede. Anybody looking at us might mistake us for lovers out for an evening stroll, she mused, which just goes to show how deceptive appearances can be.

'Not quite,' he said. 'I think if she hadn't lost the child she would have married George and got a hefty settlement for him after a year or so of misery. Australia and Charlie would have been postponed, that's all.'

'You don't happen to write fiction as a sideline, do you?' Jess scoffed.

He leant beside her and she could smell the fresh lemony aroma of his cologne. 'But all this is academic now, isn't it?' he said. 'There's no baby on the way, and Kitty's done a disappearing act, having first sold a valuable ring which was not hers to sell.'

Jess's indignation melted like ice in the sun, for no matter what she might say there was no excuse for what Kitty had done. 'She *will* pay you back.' She leaned towards him to give her words emphasis. 'You don't know Kitty. She's ... well ... she's thick, but she's not dishonest.'

However, Andros was not to be so easily convinced. 'I happen to regard selling an heirloom without permission as dishonest,' he said sternly.

'Of course it is, but Kitty's too self-centred to see that.' Her face was flushed in the effort of pleading Kitty's case, and she looked very lovely in the soft lamplight. Young and vulnerable. 'Her mother was just the same. They only see things from their point of view.'

'I really don't want to hear your family history,' he said, and although his voice was cold his eyes were not

any longer. 'The fact remains that this morning I redeemed the Kalimantis emerald for a great deal of
money.' He took a receipt from his wallet. 'This is the
amount Miss Taylor owes me.'

Jess glanced at the receipt and blanched. 'She might
have to pay in instalments,' she croaked, looking down
at the beach.

'But what guarantee do I have that I'll *ever* be repaid?'
he asked. 'Miss Taylor's rattling around somewhere in
Australia, and you——' his eyebrows drew into a straight
line '—you move around a lot. I've read your file...'

Her head shot up. 'My *what*?'

'I had a dossier made on the pair of you. You've flitted
from job to job like a flea. God knows where you'll land
next.'

She'd never done anything wrong except suffer from
restlessness, but she supposed that on a dossier so many
changes might look bad. 'There's no law against moving
about,' she said, and hated herself for sounding
defensive.

'I need collateral. As security until I'm repaid.' There
was a gleam in those dark eyes. 'You don't own any
property, do you?'

'You know damn well I don't!' she snapped.

'Well, we'll have to think of something. Perhaps you
could offer yourself?' He smiled briefly and his teeth
showed white against his dark face.

She turned on him indignantly. 'I *beg* your pardon?'

'Don't jump to conclusions,' he said airily, 'I was only
thinking of business. You know how to type, don't you?'

'Are you going to offer me a job with your company?
Keep tabs on me that way?' A gust of wind played with
the loose tendrils of her hair, and she impatiently tried
to tuck them back into her topknot, but only succeeded
in loosening more strands.

He looked at her speculatively. 'I'm working this
summer on putting a book together, translating some of

the *miroloyia* from the Deep Mani. Particularly the ones concerning any of the British who were killed during the Second World War.'

'Working on . . . what did you call them?'

'*Miroloyia*. The funeral dirges of the Mani. Long funeral hymns, sung extempore by the women. The custom's dying out now, but there are still some old women left who remember them. I plan to put them into a book. I need someone at Vathia to run things while I'm working on this. To keep the files, type and correct the manuscript. Cook and clean. I only have the summer. I need a competent girl Friday.'

She stared at him in disbelief. 'You want me to come to Vathia?'

'That's right. You could be my collateral and earn a salary at the same time.'

This is crazy, she said to herself, the man's crazy. 'Where would I live?'

He looked at her as if she wasn't very bright. 'In the tower, of course. Where else?'

'You mean...you mean you want me to *live* with you?'

'In a manner of speaking. Of course, it goes without saying that this would be strictly a business relationship—you'd share my board, but not my bed.'

'How do I know that?' she demanded. 'How do I know that you're not some kind of loony who'll rape me the moment you get me alone?'

'You don't.' He smiled. 'You'll just have to take my word that, if the lady's unwilling, I'm not about to force myself on her.'

'I can assure you I'm not in the *least* willing,' she replied with heat. 'I don't want to be rude...' She crossed her toes. Somewhere she'd read that if you crossed your toes while you told a lie you wouldn't be found out. '...but you're simply not my type.'

'Then you have nothing to worry about, have you?'

'Just the same——' she gave a disbelieving giggle '—it's crazy!'

'Of course you may have commitments here, and not want to spend the summer in Greece.' He gazed out at the glittering path made by the moonlight on the sea. 'That man you're going to meet later, for instance...'

'Oh, my God!' She jerked up her wrist and looked at her watch. 'I forgot all about Tony!'

'My car's parked further up the road, I'll drive you.' He took her arm. 'This...Tony...is he important in your life?' His voice was strangely flat.

'We're not an item—nor likely to be—if that's what you mean,' she said, and wondered if she imagined that his grip on her arm relaxed.

They approached a bottle-green Jaguar and he opened the door for her before sliding into the driver's seat. The leather seats smelled pleasantly aromatic. She told him the name of the restaurant, but before he put the car in gear he asked, 'What about your job at The Saracen's Head? Are you wedded to it?'

Honesty made her admit that she'd been thinking of making a change. 'As a matter of fact,' she confided as the car slid away from the kerb, 'I've been considering the idea of getting some more training...expanding my horizons.'

He stole a look at her as she sat beside him. In the dim light, her eyes had the shine of silver. 'That sounds like a good idea,' he said.

They left the front and headed back into town. 'How much do you make at that pub?' She told him and he nodded. 'Of course, you wouldn't have much time off if you came to Vathia to work,' he said. 'So it would only be fair to pay you more.' He mentioned a figure that made Jess's jaw drop. 'How does that sound?'

'It sounds very fair,' she gasped, doing rapid sums in her head. Why, two months' work would pay for her first semester's tuition! Then she glanced up at his rugged profile suspiciously. 'But why pay so much for just a... what was it you called me? A piece of collateral?'

'Well, I have to get somebody,' explained Andros. 'You might as well get the going rate.'

There was no way Jess could get her mind to work clearly. 'When can I let you know?' She hoped she sounded cool and businesslike, but she was sure she didn't.

He pulled up in front of the restaurant and reached into his wallet for his card. 'I'm staying in England for one more day,' he said. 'You can get me at my office.'

She peered down at the square of white cardboard. 'But why *me*?' Her chin took on a stubborn tilt. 'I mean, surely you don't want to employ me if... if you think I'm crooked.'

He leaned over her to open her door and his arm brushed lightly across her breast. A little flicker, like a mild electric jolt, went through her. 'Maybe I want to save you from a life of crime,' he said, 'guide you on to the straight and narrow.'

Her head was in far too much of a whirl to joust successfully with him. 'I'll be in touch,' she said as she climbed out of the car, 'but I'm not promising anything.'

He rolled down the window to deliver his parting shot. 'If you don't accept the job, you'll have to find me some suitable security until the debt's paid off,' he said. 'And now you'd better get a move on or your boyfriend will start sending out a search party.'

He gave her a brief salute, and the sleek car sped off into the night, leaving Jess standing on the pavement, still trying to think of a suitable rejoinder.

CHAPTER FOUR

OF COURSE, Jess decided to go. She told herself that she would be a fool to lose such an opportunity, she couldn't possibly afford to turn it down. What she didn't add was that the idea of being with Andros made her heart beat a little faster, made her breath catch in her throat. She handed in her notice at The Saracen's Head, and fourteen days later she was off to Greece.

Mrs Talbot agreed to store her few belongings in the attic, and to sub-let her room for the summer. 'Just let me know when you're coming back, lovey,' she had said, 'and the room's yours again.' And then she had fished out a pot of home-made jam from the kitchen cupboard and handed it to her favourite boarder. 'Here!' Something tasty for you. You'll need it with all that foreign food.' The Talbots had never travelled further than the Lake District, and considered *that* to be alien territory. So Jess still had a home to come back to, which gave her a nice secure feeling.

There had been a letter from Kitty, written at the same time as George's and not saying much more, except to admit that she now realised she was still in love with Charlie and was going out to find him. "I was sad when I first lost the baby, Jess," she'd written, "but now I know it is probably for the best." She hadn't mentioned a word about pawning the ring. She gets more like Aunt Mary every day, thought Jess, jamming the letter back in its envelope. But she hadn't had time to brood about Kitty's shortcomings, there was too much to do before she left, and by the time she had clambered aboard the plane for Athens it felt as if Kitty and her problems were light years away.

'Would you like to order anything from the bar?' asked the stewardess, and the man sitting in the next seat said,

'I was hoping you'd join me in a drink. To celebrate going to sunny Greece,' for it was raining again in Sussex.

She accepted a glass of wine, and the man put himself out to be charming. He was an archaeologist off to join a dig in Crete. 'Crete's a wonderful place,' he told her, and added, because she was bright and pretty, and because he was attracted to her, 'Any chance you might get over for a visit?'

She told him that there wasn't. 'I expect to have my nose pretty much to the grindstone this summer,' she replied, then she smiled, thinking that, if she judged Andros correctly, that was the understatement of all time!

When they arrived in Athens, her new friend insisted on carrying her luggage. As arranged, Andros was waiting for her by the barrier. 'Oh,' said the archaeologist, 'is that your husband meeting you?'

'My *boss*,' she said firmly. She found a certain exhilaration at the idea of meeting Andros in the company of a nice-looking man rather than creeping into Athens alone, so she said, 'Come on, I'll introduce you.'

Apart from raising one dark eyebrow the merest fraction of an inch, Andros was the soul of courtesy. The three of them chatted for a few moments, but before her plane companion took his leave he scribbled his address on a piece of paper and handed it to Jess. 'Just in case you do get a chance to visit,' he said, 'remember I'll always be happy to see you.'

'Friend of yours?' remarked Andros as he walked away.

'Could be.' She tucked the paper into her handbag. 'He wants me to visit him in Crete.'

'Not a hope!' Andros lifted her suitcase with one hand and hoisted the strap of her flight-bag on to his shoulder. 'You're here to work, not go chasing after men.'

'Just for the record,' she informed him loftily, 'I don't chase after men.'

'I can believe that,' he agreed, 'but you'd better reconcile yourself to the fact that you're here to work on my book... not your social life!'

He piled her luggage into the boot of his car, and held the door open for her. 'All right with you if we leave the sunroof open?' he asked, and without waiting for her answer he climbed into the driver's seat and started the engine.

Jess took a scarlet cotton scarf from her bag and tied it over her hair. 'Would it make any difference if it wasn't?' she enquired demurely.

He grinned at her and said, 'Nope!' and because she was suddenly filled with an irrational glow of happiness she grinned back.

He took the road to Sparta, driving fast and expertly without wasting time in conversation. She didn't mind the silence. She was starting the most exciting summer of her twenty-three years; she didn't need conversation.

They stopped finally at the seaport town of Yithion for a meal. 'This is a good place to eat,' said Andros, parking the car beside a taverna on the waterfront. It faced a little island that was attached to the mainland by a long narrow mole. 'They have good fish here. Do you like fish?'

Jess climbed out of the car, stretching her long legs and smoothing the creases out of her cream slacks. She untied her scarf to let her hair swing loose, like a hank of heavy silk, and as he led the way to a table that faced the sea she told him she liked fish very much. 'You won't find me hard to feed,' she promised.

He loosened his tie. He was wearing a light summer suit, but he had removed the jacket and had rolled up the sleeves of his fine lawn shirt. The dark hairs glinted along his arms in the sunlight, and she could see the dark outline of the hair on his chest.

He examined the menu. 'Taramosalata followed by grilled swordfish—how does that sound?'

'Fine,' she nodded. She was very hungry.

A waiter took their order and left them a small basket of good Greek bread still warm from the oven. When Andros took a slice, she noticed that his nails were nicely manicured, although his hands looked as if they were not unused to hard work. He put a piece of bread in his mouth, and she found herself admiring those firm, well modelled lips of his. It would be nice to be kissed by lips like that, to feel his moustache brushing against her mouth. It would feel incredibly sexy! Hastily, she turned her attention to the plastic salt-shaker and studied it intently.

There was a short silence, during which she was uncomfortably aware that her cheeks were burning before he surprised her by asking, 'Is your hair naturally that colour?'

Taken off guard she stammered, 'Ye—yes.'

'Incredible! Like precious metal.' He made a move, as if he were going to reach out and touch her glossy mane, but at that moment the waiter arrived with their first course.

The fish pâté was good, piquant and salty, but Jess's mind was not on the food. She was grappling with the thought that the next few weeks were going to prove something of a strain if Andros was going to start touching her... unless she decided to accept his caresses and the inevitable consequence, but that didn't seem like a very good idea. Better to keep him at arm's length. She mustn't lose sight of the fact that she was here with him as security for a debt; allowing herself to become involved would be unwise.

He had ordered a carafe of retsina and now he poured her a glass. 'I hope you like it,' he said. 'Retsina's an acquired taste.'

'I love it.' She took a sip and the wine tingled pleasantly on her palate.

'There are many legends about retsina,' he said, holding the glass of golden liquid to the light. 'One of them is that, when the Persians were invading Athens, the people tried to save their wine from the invaders by adding resin from pine trees to the wine to make it taste bad, but when they reopened the jars they were delighted with the flavour, and they've been drinking it ever since. Most Greeks will tell you that, not only is retsina good for you, it will never give you a hangover.'

'I don't think I'll test that theory,' smiled Jess, 'I'll take their word for it.'

The waiter arrived balancing plates, and the enticing aroma of grilled fish filled her nostrils. She picked up her knife and fork eagerly. They ate in silence for a while. When they'd finished, Andros ordered coffee and asked for the bill.

'I insist on paying for my share of the meal,' she said firmly.

'Don't be stupid, Jess.' He took some drachma notes out of his wallet.

'I'm not being stupid,' she insisted, 'just independent.' And playing safe, she might have added; this is beginning to feel like a date.

'Since I'll be feeding you anyway, this doesn't count as a dinner date,' he said, and she wondered if he could read her mind.

'Nevertheless...'

He leaned forward and looked straight into her mutinous grey eyes. 'Let's get one thing straight right now. *I'm* running this show. If I say I'm paying for your meals, that's the way it's going to be...understood?'

'Yes, *sir*, Mr. Kalimantis,' she snarled. He might be a sexy man, but he was also the most domineering man she'd ever met. She had a strong desire to hit him.

'And you'd better start calling me Andros,' he told her, 'I'd prefer it.'

'You're the boss!' she said in a low, fierce voice.

'As long as you understand that, we'll have no trouble.' He looked at her coolly and she glared at him and then determinedly looked away and studied the little island while she sipped her coffee.

'I see that you're fascinated by the island,' he said after a while. 'It has quite a history.'

She could hear the smile in his voice and this did nothing to restore her good humour. 'Really!'

It was a flat statement, not a question, but he went on, '*Really!* It used to be called Kranai. It's supposed to be the island where Paris and Helen spent the first night of their illicit honeymoon after he carried her off.'

Jess said, 'The way you're carrying me?' and then she blushed so hard she thought her cheeks would scorch, because the last thing they were doing was taking off on a honeymoon.

His eyebrows shot up. 'Carrying you? I believe you came of your own free will.'

'Yes...of course...' And to prevent further discussion, she said, 'Perhaps you should start telling me what my duties will be when we get to Vathia.'

'Wouldn't you rather talk about Paris and Helen couched in love upon the sweet-smelling fennel?' Andros asked with a devilish glint in his eyes.

'No, I wouldn't!' She turned away again, almost knocking her coffee-cup over.

'I thought all women liked romance,' he observed.

'Well, *I* don't.' Damn him! He was playing with her like a cat with a mouse.

'What a pity. However, I'm not sure I believe you. I believe that somewhere under that tough exterior a warm human being is lurking.'

'Shouldn't we be getting on?' she said. 'Otherwise it will be dark before we know it.' He gave a sardonic chuckle and, having paid the bill, led the way from the taverna.

Once they were back in the car she sat slewed in her seat, with as much of her back towards him as was humanly possible. To their right, the great spine of the Taiyetos mountains swam with shadows, and after a while Andros turned the car in that direction and headed for the Messenian Gulf coastal road.

After a spectacular sunset, which she learned later was not an unusual phenomenon in these parts, it soon became dark. Seen through the open sun-roof, the stars looked like shards of crystal hanging in the velvet sky. The air had cooled down, and it blew against her face, fragrant with the scent of the sea. It was a different kind of sea-tang from the Sussex coast, though, a softer, more voluptuous air that enfolded her like a cloak of silk.

After a time, the unnatural position she'd twisted herself into became unbearable, so she eased herself round and lay back in her seat. She could just make out Andros's face in the light from the dashboard. His unruly hair had fallen over his forehead, and the shadows exaggerated the two deep lines that bracketed his mouth. His concentration was entirely on the winding road before him, he seemed oblivious to the girl at his side. Finally she drifted off into sleep and only woke when he was driving up the peaked height that led to Vathia. The dashboard clock registered eleven. The village was shuttered and silent. The headlights sliced through the night and glared for a moment on the wall that surrounded his tower. He turned off the lights and the engine, and the sounds of the night whispered around them. 'Home at last,' he said softly.

She stumbled out of the car and stood looking up at the inky mass of mountains that soared above. The wind soughed through the jungle of prickly pear. The only other sounds were the shrill note of some crickets, and a faint chorus of frogs, which hinted at water somewhere in this parched landscape. There wasn't a light to be seen in any of the towers. It was like a dead village; she and Andros could have been the only people left on earth, and she trembled with an irrational fear as she watched his tall shadow lifting her luggage from the car.

Silently, he unlatched the gate and led the way into his strange domain, his feet echoing loudly on the paving stones. There was a jangle of keys, and with a reluctant groan the low door opened. The interior was so black, it looked like a painted square on the wall of the tower.

'Wait till I get us some light,' he said, disappearing into the darkness. A match flared, and light, the colour of yellow wine, flowed from an oil lamp that stood on the wooden table. Carefully he replaced the glass shade. 'Come in,' he said to the hesitant girl, 'but leave the door open. It's musty in here.'

She stumbled over her case and would have fallen if he hadn't put out his arm to steady her. His hand felt warm through the cotton of her shirt, but all the same she shivered at his touch.

'I think we should go straight to bed,' he said.

'Wh...what?' she stammered through lips that had grown dry with apprehension.

He peered down into her face, his eyes inscrutable. 'You sleep on the top floor,' he told her with a faint smile. 'It's really a store-room, but I've put a camp bed in there. You should be comfortable enough.'

'Oh! Yes... Fine, that'll be fine!' she babbled, and she heard him give a soft chuckle.

He lit another lamp and handed it to her. 'Go on ahead and I'll bring up your luggage.'

The storeroom was the one with the packing cases. These had been pushed to one side and now a small bed, and a table with a basin and a jug on it, stood in their place.

'We'll have to fix up a place for your clothes tomorrow,' he said. 'And I'm afraid there's no water either till the morning—when I go to the pump.'

'It doesn't matter,' she mumbled, although she hadn't realised it would be *quite* so primitive.

'I can give you a bottle of water for your teeth, though!' Again he seemed to guess her thoughts. 'Things aren't quite that bad.'

She went over to the bed. It was unmade, with two single sheets and a light blanket neatly folded on the end. 'This will be fine,' she said to his retreating back.

While he was gone she unpacked her nightie and sponge-bag and made up the bed, and when he returned she was vigorously brushing her hair.

'Here you are!' He put the bottle of water and a toothmug down on the table. 'All set?'

She looked up, her face rosy from the effort of brushing. 'There's not much air in here,' she said. 'Those things don't open wider, do they?' She pointed her brush at the long, narrow windows.

'Easily fixed.' He went to the trapdoor above their heads and shot the bolt, flinging it open. A faint patch of star-studded sky became visible. 'I only close this when it rains, and it doesn't do that very often.'

A faint breath of wind at once wafted into the circular room and Jess said, 'Vathia's version of air-conditioning?' and he grinned.

'That reminds me,' he said, climbing up the ladder and disappearing on to the roof. After a moment he leaned down, his wide shoulders blocking the view of the sky. 'Here! Take these.' He handed her down two heavy cannon balls.

'What on earth . . .' She put them on the floor. When he had come back into the room she asked, 'Are we about to start a war?'

'Those, my dear, are your protection!' She looked at him blankly. 'You simply put those things on to your trapdoor once I've left you. By the time I've shoved my way into your room, these will be thundering about like cannon-shot and you'll have plenty of time to defend yourself against my advances.'

'I thought you only advanced if the lady was willing,' she reminded him.

'How do you know I wasn't lying?' he teased. 'Now, goodnight! See you in the morning.' And he retreated down the ladder, pulling the trapdoor shut.

After a moment's hesitation, Jess rolled the cannon balls on top of it. She felt a little silly, but she wasn't sure she trusted him. Come to that, she wasn't sure she trusted herself to resist him if he turned on the charm, so much good the cannon balls would do! But at least it was a gesture.

After she'd brushed her teeth, she lay on top of the bed and looked up at the sky, enjoying the sweet air which had quickly chased away the musty, locked-up atmosphere.

My fortress, she thought sleepily, for the circular brick walls and narrow embrasures did have the appearance of a castle tower. With my brave knight keeping guard beneath me . . . And the thought of Andros, lying in his bed, with just a few feet of stone between them, made her blood beat in her veins. With an irritated sigh at her weak-mindedness, she turned on her side and fell asleep.

Andros was nowhere around when she got up and dressed the next morning. It was early, not yet six, and the sky was washed with lemon-coloured light from the pale new sun. Jess stood in the kitchen, tucking her pink shirt into the waist of a pair of white shorts, her mass of heavy blonde hair still tousled from her pillow. She wandered over to a very new-looking kitchen sink and turned on the single tap. Nothing happened.

'It's not connected yet,' said Andros from the doorway. 'We're going to fix it after breakfast.'

She whirled round in surprise, losing one of her flip-flop sandals in the process. 'You startled me!'

'Give me a hand, will you?' He passed her a dish with eggs in it, and a loaf of bread that was almost hot, it was so soon out of the oven. 'We can always buy bread and eggs from the taverna,' he informed her. 'Later on, we'll go into Yerolimin for supplies.'

He went outside again and reappeared carrying a cooking-pot full of water. 'I've only brought enough water for now,' he said.

'What can I do?' she asked.

'Make breakfast, of course.' He put the pot of water by a primus stove and headed outside again. 'You'll find powdered coffee in the cupboard.'

Charming! Jess thought as she foraged about in the cupboard. It might have been nice if he'd offered to at least *show* me where things were to be found on my first morning.

She found coffee and a small saucepan to boil water in, but the primus stove gave her difficulty, and after struggling with it without success she went out into the yard for help.

Andros was carrying a length of copper pipe and he looked none too pleased when she approached him. 'Yes! What is it?'

'The stove... I can't get it to work.' She held out the matches. 'I'm terrified of blowing us up.'

'You'd better get un-terrified,' he said. 'I won't always be here to do it for you.'

'Perhaps if you could give me a lesson?' she suggested with a sweetness she was far from feeling. She rattled the match-box.

He took the box and came into the kitchen. 'Now,' he said, 'watch carefully! You have to pump it first.' The stove lit with a baleful roar and he adjusted the flame. 'Is that all? We've got a lot to do today, and we're late starting.'

Jess, who had never thought of six a.m. as late, said, 'Just one other thing...where's the milk for the coffee?'

'There isn't any. I like my coffee black.'

She hated black coffee first thing, but she bit her tongue and asked, 'Boiled eggs? Or fried?

When Andros answered shortly, 'Boiled...fried... whatever. It doesn't matter,' and went outside again, she satisfied herself by making a rude gesture in the direction he'd taken.

It took her a long time to prepare their simple meal because she had to search for every utensil before she could get going, but finally the eggs were ready, and the coffee made, and she called him in.

She had boiled the eggs, and she had done them the way *she* liked them. If he was going to be so cavalier about the milk, she felt she was entitled to that satisfaction, and since he ate three without complaint she assumed they met with his approval.

When they'd finished, he said, 'You can't do the washing up till we have water, so I want you to help me to connect the new electric pump.'

She stood up meekly. 'Very well!'

He looked her over. Her long legs were smooth as ivory, and her shorts gleamed in the dim room. 'For God's sake!' he said. 'Didn't you bring any work clothes with you?'

'*You're* wearing shorts,' she pointed out. He was wearing his frayed khaki shorts again, teamed this morning with a disreputable T-shirt full of holes.

'You look as if you're off to some trendy picnic,' he said. 'Don't you have jeans?'

She had jeans in her luggage. 'Yes,' she said, heading for the ladder, 'I'll change.'

'And put on a pair of proper shoes,' he yelled after her, 'those flip-flop things are *useless* in the Mani. It's rocky here, or hadn't you noticed?'

She put on old jeans and a pair of sneakers and returned downstairs. By now she was beginning to get fed up with being ordered around in such an autocratic way, but she was determined not to lose her temper. As he'd pointed out, he was the boss, so the hired help had better keep her mouth shut.

'Here I am,' she said, tying her hair back with a piece of ribbon. 'What can I do?'

'You can hand me tools as I need them.' A blow-torch and a box of tools were on the floor by his side. 'And you can clean up under the sink while I'm hooking up the piping. You'll find a dustpan and brush by the cupboard.'

'Sure!' And then she couldn't resist saying, 'Any rocks you want split while I'm about it?' but he didn't smile.

While he worked on the piping, Jess crouched under the sink and attempted to clean about a hundred years of grime and mouse droppings from the dank recess. Every time he barked out an order for a tool, she would bang her head, or scrape an elbow against the rough stone wall. Cobwebs clung to her face and she had to bite on her lip to stop herself from screaming, for she was terrified of spiders. Grimly she swept and swabbed, and all the while she cursed him silently.

They worked steadily, and by nine they were finished. By now Jess was filthy. Her hair was covered in cobwebs, three of her fingernails were broken, and the sweat was running down her body. She knew she was going to ache in every muscle by the evening, but she still didn't complain, although it was on the tip of her tongue to remark that this was a funny kind of typing.

Andros looked at his watch. He'd stripped off his T-shirt, and the muscles on his back were oiled with sweat. He looked like a beautiful copper statue. Too bad his personality doesn't match his body, Jess thought sourly.

'I'll just run some water and we can have a wash, then we'll drive into Yerolimin for groceries,' he said.

'Yes, sir.' She pulled on her forelock which was lank with perspiration. 'What else?'

'You can clear up here while I'm washing, then you can have a wash too. You look as if you need one. Now let's get a move on, or everything will be closed.'

While she tidied up the kitchen, Andros splashed water happily into the sink. 'It works, Jess!' he called out. 'I'm a bloody genius!'

'And I didn't do a thing, of course!' she muttered under her breath, but biting back her resentment she said, 'Congratulations. You'll get the Nobel prize at this rate!'

After she had had a delicious wash in the cold water, and brushed most of the cobwebs out of her hair, they drove off to Yerolimin.

In the car, she stretched out her legs—she'd changed back into her shorts—and winced at the muscle pain in her calves.

'What's wrong?' He glanced down at her.

'Oh, nothing! I'm just crippled, that's all.'

'Sorry if I've been riding you hard,' he said, 'but I don't want you to get the idea that this is a holiday in sunny Greece.'

'A holiday!' she protested. 'I don't usually spend my holidays crawling about under sinks.'

'The view was nice though,' he said, and when she looked surprised he added, 'For me. You have a very attractive rear-end.'

She could feel the colour start from the base of her throat to the roots of her golden hair, while she stared mutely at the rocky landscape, furious that, as usual when Andros admired her, she seemed reduced to a blushing idiot.

'I've got some business to attend to in Yerolimin,' he said cheerfully, 'so if you want an hour to yourself, feel free to go sightseeing.'

'Thank you.' An hour away from his overpowering presence might not be a bad idea.

He parked the car by the little grocery store that also did service as a post office. 'Let's synchronise our watches.' He held his sun bronzed wrist next to her slim one. 'One hour from now, we'll meet here. And don't be late. I don't like to be kept waiting.'

She pulled her straw sunhat down over her eyes. 'Who does?' she said severely. She was getting fed-up with his peremptory orders. She supposed it went with being a high-powered executive.

'See you later, then!' he said, and they went their separate ways.

Jess loved to explore, and the little town of Yerolimin delighted her. She prowled its streets and admired its substantial merchants' houses, shabby now but still handsome, built at a time when this sleepy little place was an important trading centre in Greece. She discovered an enchanting little colonnaded square with tall palm trees and statues, and a rakish little bandstand that had an air of battered gaiety about it. She had a cup of coffee at one of the old-fashioned cafés and bought a box of Turkish Delight to send to the Talbots, before wandering back to the harbour where the fishermen moored their boats, and where occasionally a pleasure cruiser would tie up for a day or two.

As she walked along the quay, she could see Andros's tall figure waiting for her and she quickened her pace.

'You're not late,' he said as she came up to him, 'don't panic.'

'I'm not panicking,' she replied with more sharpness than she intended. 'I know very well I'm not late.' She was annoyed to discover that as soon as she'd spied him her heart had given a little leap of pleasure. She had thought she had more control over her reactions.

Nevertheless, shopping with Andros was fun. Everybody in the store seemed to know him, and although she couldn't follow the conversation she enjoyed listening to him chatting with the locals, and she found herself joining in the laughter, even though she didn't really understand the jokes.

He bought a large supply of tinned food, and fresh vegetables and fruit, as well as several bottles of ouzo and a case of wine. Then they visited the butcher. 'I usually eat at a taverna,' he said, 'but if you can handle a roast of lamb we might eat in tonight.'

She had a moment's alarm, remembering the tower's primitive kitchen, but she agreed cheerily enough, having made sure that they bought a roasting pan. Finally, laden with purchases, they drove back to Vathia just as the town was closing for the siesta.

Andros helped her unpack, and he cut bread and unwrapped a slab of local cheese while she prepared a green salad. Jess made a good salad, and she was glad to see that he had two liberal helpings. If she had the same success with tonight's lamb, all would be well.

They ate at the kitchen table, and over their coffee—to her relief, he had bought milk—she asked about Vathia and the towers.

'It's such a funny place,' she said. 'I mean, why *towers*? Why not ordinary houses?'

'The Maniots built towers here, and in other places in the Mani, because of local wars,' he said.

Her eyes, which appeared gun-metal grey in the shadowy room, opened wide. 'Local *wars*?'

'That's right. The Mani was known for its feuds, so they built these towers and clobbered each other.'

'Do you mean to tell me that the village was *divided*? A little place like this?' He nodded and she gave a laugh of disbelief. 'But some of the towers are only a few metres apart. It's crazy!'

'Well, people from the Mani *are* crazy, sometimes, and proud—and sometimes quarrelsome,' he said, reaching for an orange and starting to peel it.

She looked at him speculatively. 'Do you come from here originally?'

'My father did. But the family moved to Athens when he was small. He always used to come back to visit his village, though.'

'This village?'

'This village. And I thought it would be fun to have a place here. Get in touch with my roots.'

'I should think you'd feel right at home surrounded by an arsenal of cannon balls,' she remarked drily. 'Barking orders and attacking people seems to come naturally to you.'

'I only attack verbally,' he said. 'I wouldn't dream of throwing things.'

Still curious, Jess asked, 'But that's what those cannon balls on the roof were for? For hurling at the neighbours?'

He handed her a section of orange, but she refused. Handing her pieces of his food in this cosy way was a bit too intimate for safety.

'I must say, knowing something of your heritage sheds quite a light on your personality,' she remarked acidly.

'Which I gather is not to your liking.' He played with a piece of the peel on his plate.

Jess shrugged with deliberate indifference. 'I'm only an employee,' she said airily. 'It doesn't really matter what I think.'

'I can assure you that I'm really a charmer.' His eyes crinkled up attractively as he grinned. 'Even if my forebears were pirates.'

She stopped in the act of lifting her coffee-cup. 'Are you serious?'

'Of course. Piracy was a going concern for the Maniots back in the seventeenth century. Anybody who comes from around here is bound to have a pirate or two among his ancestors.'

'I believe you,' she told him. 'Ever since I met you I've pictured you with a gold ear-ring and an eye-patch.'

'How about a wooden leg as well? I must say, you're not very flattering.'

'Is that what you want from me? Flattery?' she said, and then wished she hadn't because it sounded flirtatious.

'I want...' He threw the piece of peel back on to his plate. 'I'd *like*...to rid my mind of all suspicion, Jess.' He wasn't playing jokey games any more, he was serious.

'About Kitty and me?' she asked flatly. 'About black-mailing George?'

He didn't answer her directly, but said softly, 'I wish with all my heart we'd met under different circumstances.'

She got up and started to collect their lunch dishes with much clattering of china.

'I must say,' she snapped, filling the kettle noisily, 'your obsession about blackmail verges on paranoia.'

'No doubt.' He took the matches from her and lit the stove. 'As I've said before...I have reasons.'

When the final plate had been rinsed, she asked him for the notes he wanted copied. 'I mustn't waste any more time,' she said abruptly, because his suspicions still rankled.

'Don't be ridiculous, Jess, it's much too hot to work. Go up and have a siesta, that's what I'm going to do. You can work tonight after dinner, if you want.'

It *was* hot. Even in the tower, with its thick walls and slotted windows, the air was sultry. But Jess pushed her hair back from her sticky forehead and said crossly, 'You brought me here to work, didn't you? Why not collect your pound of flesh?'

'There won't be any flesh to collect, it'll have melted away. And I don't want you tapping away on the typewriter while I'm trying to sleep, so stop being difficult.'

'I'm not used to sleeping during the day,' she insisted sulkily.

'Then *read* for God's sake!' He rose and headed for the ladder. 'I don't give a damn what you do, just don't make a noise.'

She scuttled after him then, because it suddenly dawned on her that to get to her room for a book she would have to go through *his* room. And she didn't want to do that when he was stretched out, possibly naked, on his bed.

When they reached his floor, he stripped off his shirt and threw it on a cane chair. 'Not going to whitewash the kitchen in your spare time?' he enquired as she began to climb again. 'It needs doing.'

She didn't reply, partly because she was cross with him, but mainly because the sight of his broad brown chest made her want to lean against it and run her hands through his mat of black hair, and in the grip of this desire she didn't trust herself to speak.

Once in her room, she peeled off her shorts and shirt, and then because she felt so hot, she removed her bra as well. She'd bought a new Ruth Rendell at Gatwick and now she lay on her bed and opened it, but it was too hot to concentrate. The patch of sky, framed in the square of the trapdoor, was almost silver it was so clear, and she fancied she could *see* the heat throbbing in the transparent air. The only sound was the distant buzz of a million cicadas in the motionless afternoon. The book fell from her hand and slowly, in spite of all her protests, she drifted into a deep sleep.

CHAPTER FIVE

THE rattle of a metal can woke Jess. Andros's head was poking up through the trapdoor in her floor. Oh, God! She'd forgotten to close and put the cannon balls on it!

'Two cans of water—one hot, one cold,' he said, lifting them and placing them effortlessly on the floor.

'Th . . . thank you.' She sat up, grabbing for the sheet and holding it in front of her to cover her nearly naked body. 'Wh . . . what time is it?'

'It's just four. Relax!' He seemed amused by her struggle with the sheet. 'I'll leave you to it. If you need more water, give a yell.'

His freshly combed head disappeared down the ladder and she leapt off the bed, still swathed in her sheet, and slammed the trapdoor shut.

By juggling the cans, she was able to shampoo her hair as well, so that when she went downstairs, dressed in a favourite skirt that was striped with scarlet and teal, and a clean teal-blue shirt tucked into a wide belt, she felt human again. But very self-conscious.

'What do I do about the dirty water?' she asked, and Andros told her that he would go and empty it from the roof.

All this carrying of water seemed an unnecessary chore, and she asked if it would be more convenient if in future she washed downstairs at the sink.

'Convenient, yes,' he agreed, 'but less private.' He regarded her quizzically. 'You seemed rather disturbed when I arrived like Aquarius with my water jugs.'

'Nonsense!' She gave a bright, false smile. 'You woke me up, that's all.'

'Your privacy shall be sacrosanct,' he assured her. 'I'll take long walks during your ablutions.' He smiled crookedly. 'Even in the rain!'

Thinking it was high time to change the subject, Jess remarked, 'I'd better do something about that lamb.' She was feeling ridiculously shy and had to fight the urge to babble—a habit of hers when she was nervous.

'First, I must light a fire in the pit,' he said, and she stopped in her tracks.

'Pit?'

'Well, there's no stove here—that's my next project—but the previous owner built a sort of barbecue just outside the walls. There's a spit, too.'

'Oh!' She looked at him unenthusiastically. 'Who's going to turn it?'

'We are, of course,' he informed her. 'Don't make a face, we'll take turns.'

While he made a fire, Jess did what she could with the leg of lamb, rubbing the outside of it with some rosemary she found in one of the cupboards, and pushing slivers of garlic under the skin. It seemed awfully big for the two of them; it looked as if they would be eating cold lamb for a long time!

They had a lot of difficulty fixing the joint on to the spit. No matter how they tried, it seemed to be top-heavy, and *then* they had a struggle putting the spit, with its burden of raw meat, over the fire. Fat kept hissing out of it, and flames leapt up alarmingly, blackening the surface but not cooking it.

Jess was standing watching during most of this operation, for it was dirty work and she wasn't keen on getting her clothes covered in hot lamb fat.

Andros was starting to use bad language, swearing at the joint that was revolving in a lop-sided manner, struggling to right it when it wobbled like a drunken ballet dancer executing a difficult pirouette.

Jess could feel the laughter welling up inside her. Just at that moment the apparatus gave a long-drawn-out squeak, shuddered, and the whole thing collapsed, dropping the meat into the fire-pit. Andros jumped back as flames leaped up, and then dashed into the kitchen for water, returning to throw the contents of a full bucket on the flames. Now there was only smoke from the pit in which nestled their nearly raw and blackened dinner.

'Bon appetit!' he said, staring down at the mess.

Jess gave up trying to suppress her hilarity and collapsed in a gale of laughter and after a moment Andros joined in, taking her in his arms so that they clung together, the tears pouring down their cheeks.

'Our dinner,' she gasped clinging to him. 'Oh, Andros...our beautiful dinner!'

He brushed a strand of hair off her cheek and their laughter stopped as suddenly as it had begun, but he didn't release her. She was so close to him she could feel the heat generated by his powerful body, smell the cottony perfume of his freshly laundered shirt.

She looked away, her dark lashes fanning against her cheek. She heard him murmur in a voice that was soft as a sigh, 'Jess...' Just when he seemed about to bend his head to kiss her, she pushed firmly against his chest and said loudly, 'What do we do for food?'

After a fraction of a pause, he let her go. 'The taverna,' he said. 'Tonight we eat out.'

He washed the soot off his hands and also washed the hapless leg of lamb and put it in a plastic bag. It was to be a gift for the old woman who owned the taverna and who possessed the unlikely name of Aphrodite.

'Her barbecue's better than ours,' said Andros.

'It couldn't be worse,' Jess replied, but neither of them laughed. The laughter had gone out of them since he'd held her in his arms and she had been just a kiss away from surrender.

They set out for the taverna and he took her arm and guided her down the steep dirt track. 'There are only about thirty folk living in Vathia now,' he said, 'and they're all quite elderly.' She sensed that he was making conversation because of the awkwardness that now lay between them. 'The young people left a while ago. There's nothing in the Mani for them, except hardship.'

He started telling her a little of the history of this strange part of Greece, but she hardly heard him. His touch on her arm, his warm body so close to hers, blocked out everything else, and she was filled with that sense of dread that always attacked her when she felt in danger of becoming emotionally involved.

They reached the village, and here the towers were built close together and rose in a bewildering complex of sky-scrapers from the maze of cobbled streets. Sometimes the cobbled path became a series of shallow stairs, slippery from years of use, and then Andros's grip on her arm would tighten and she would be forced to lean against him. She wondered if he could feel the beating of her heart, for it felt as if it might break her ribs, it thudded so hard.

At the taverna, it looked as if the same old men were sitting in the same chairs under the plane trees, chatting in their strange Maniot dialect, slipping amber worry beads through gnarled sun-browned fingers.

'Let's have a cold beer,' Andros said, leading her to an empty table. Aphrodite tottered out to take their order and Andros presented her with the lamb.

She brought them two ice-cold bottles of beer and then, with a knowing glance at Jess, she asked him a question.

He laughed and shook his dark head. *'Ochi!'* he said, which Jess knew was the word for 'no'.

The woman shook her head and drew her lips back in a toothless grin. She said something to the old men, who eyed Jess curiously.

'Whoo, Andros!' croaked one. 'Bravo!' And they all laughed and slapped their withered thighs.

'What are they saying?' Jess asked.

'They're complimenting me on having such a beautiful secretary,' said Andros, smooth as satin.

'Are you sure they understand I'm just a secretary?' She was beginning to have an inkling of what this nodding and thigh slapping was all about.

He grinned. 'Well...no. I tried to explain to Aphrodite, but she refused to believe me.'

'They all think I'm your mistress, don't they?' she demanded, feeling unreasonably angry.

'Yes, they do, but they all think you're gorgeous. I don't know why you're getting so upset.'

'Because it's not true.'

'What's not true? That you're gorgeous?'

'The mistress bit!' she snapped. 'Don't play games. I came here to help you with your typing and your silly tower. I'm not being driven into your bed by a bunch of dirty old men.' She glared at the offending ancients.

'That conjures up quite a picture,' he drawled. She took a sip of beer and choked, and he said sharply, 'For God's sake, relax, girl! You've been as tense as a strung wire ever since we...we burnt our dinner.' His jet eyes were opaque, unreadable. 'There's nothing to be tense about. Your virtue's quite safe, so stop making such a fuss about a bunch of harmless old men.'

'I don't enjoy being gossiped about,' muttered Jess defensively, but in her heart she knew that this was not the real reason. She was upset because she was discovering that he just had to touch her for her heart to turn over with desire, and the strength of this emotion frightened her.

She did not enjoy her dinner that evening, although it was good. The stewed chicken was succulent, the fried potatoes appetising, and the salad crisp. It was not fancy, and there was no choice. In this establishment you got what was available, there was nothing as sophisticated as a menu, but the food was well cooked and plentiful, and normally she would have relished it.

When they returned to the tower, she spent the rest of the evening reading through the *miroloyia* that Andros had translated.

'Here!' He dumped another pile of folders on the table. 'This should keep you busy for the couple of days that I'm away.'

She looked up from the page she was studying, her hair gleaming in the lamplight as if it had been polished. 'Are you going away?'

'In search of more material. That's why I hired you, so I could get away.'

'Of course,' she replied dully, and wondered why she felt disappointed. She should be feeling pleased that the source of such turmoil was going to be absent. But, next morning, when he came clumping down the ladder in his hiking boots, a full backpack slung over his shoulder, she still felt downcast.

After breakfast, he asked if she could drive, and when she said she could be handed her the car keys. 'You might as well have these, then,' he said. 'If you get stir-crazy, or need anything, you can go for a drive.'

Jess was surprised. 'You trust me to drive your car?'

'It's rented!' he replied with a smile. 'But I don't think you'll wreck it. You strike me as a cautious young woman.' And she knew he was not just referring to her driving.

'I thought I struck you as a crook,' she said, industriously sweeping crumbs off the kitchen table.

'An *incipient* crook,' he corrected. 'That's not quite the same thing.'

Her face hardened. 'It's the same thing to me!'

He replied, very softly, 'Maybe I was mistaken.'

'You're damn right you were,' she snorted, but her spirits rose a little at this confession.

'I'd better be off.' He went out into the yard, pulling the pack on to his powerful shoulders. She followed him. 'When you've finished typing up that stuff, you should take a break—have a swim, or go for a walk.'

'Thank you!' she said ironically, knowing she had a good two days' slogging ahead of her.

He jammed a battered linen hat on to his head. 'I should be back in two days—three, at the most.' He appeared uncharacteristically irresolute. 'If there's any kind of emergency, you can always call the Athens office. The number's on my desk.'

'All right!' she laughed. 'Now, get going! Otherwise it'll be time for lunch.' For a moment she thought he was going to kiss her cheek, and she imperceptibly backed away, but he merely saluted briefly, turned on his heel and left.

The tower seemed strangely silent when she went back inside, as if the heart had gone out of it. It wasn't that she was lonely, exactly, but she felt at a loose end, even with that mountain of typing to do. She kept imagining that she heard him. That maybe he'd forgotten something, or decided not to go, after all. But he didn't come back for three days.

She had finished the typing, tidied the kitchen cupboards, and taken her first drive in the rented Mercedes before he marched in at sunset, with three days' growth of beard on his face and a full tape deck to be translated and copied.

She was inordinately pleased to see him, but managed to hide her pleasure in the bustle of heating water for him to wash and shave, and preparing a light supper so they wouldn't have to go out.

He stayed for four days, long enough to translate the contents of his tape recorder, then he was off again, toiling up into the mountains, his sturdy boots ringing on the sun-baked rock.

This more or less became the pattern of her life in Vathia. For days at a time she would be alone, typing and filing, keeping notes, tidying the tower. And then Andros would come back, and it was as if the sun had come from behind a cloud. Ruefully, she reflected that she need not have worried that she might fall into his bed. His bed always seemed to be empty! Just as well, she decided, much safer this way. Gives me time to recover from my infatuation. But still, when she heard him call, 'Anybody home?' she had to guard herself not to dash out to him and fling herself into his arms.

The time that he was with her became precious to Jess. Every night at sundown they would drink a glass of ouzo on the roof of the tower and admire the sunset. She remembered that this was just as she had found him that first evening. Little did she dream then that she would be sharing such moments with him!

He would teach her a few phrases of Greek, and she would studiously copy them into a notebook to memorise later, for she was anxious to learn the language.

It was immeasurably peaceful up there, sitting on the little cane-covered chairs that he had hauled up to go with the tin table. Since his tower was at the highest point, the other towers were invisible. They might have been sitting on a magic carpet in the soft evening light which turned the harsh mountains above them to golden and lavender. Just she and Andros...alone in the world! It was the only time during the day that she relaxed her guard. Most of the time she was as cautious with him as a wild colt.

When she was on her own she began to explore, taking time to pick her way through the jungle of cactus and prickly pear to the higher reaches, and to sit on a slab of rock, looking back at the village of towers below.

She managed to strike up a relationship of sorts with the woman who did their laundry: a middle-aged giantess, who pounded their garments vigorously in a stone trough before laying them out to dry on boulders and cactus branches. Their conversations were necessarily brief, since they were carried on mainly with the aid of Jess's phrase-book, and the few words she had learnt from Andros, but it was friendly, and usually ended with them sharing a cup of milk and a handful of roasted chick peas.

On one excursion, she found the source of the nightly frog chorus. Wandering along a goat track, she discovered a cleft in the limestone mountainside that was filled with green plane trees and figs and sycamores. There were pink and white oleanders, too, and a tinkling thread of water that fell from the rockface into a depression in the rock, creating a pool that fluttered with water-weeds. She sipped the water, and it was so cold that it made her teeth ache. She gathered some of the oleanders to brighten up the kitchen, and all the way home she happily made plans to have a picnic when Andros came back.

She discovered a marvellous place to swim. It was a steep climb down the cliff-face but it was worth it, for at the bottom was a ledge of rock surrounded by a deep blue pool. It was a blue-green paradise. Shaded from the fierce sun, the water was deep and cool. She never saw a soul and soon grew confident enough to swim naked and afterwards to lie staring down at the grottoes and canyons in the pool while the salt dried to silver on her firm young body.

She'd been living at the tower for six weeks when she decided to whitewash the kitchen. Andros had gone off on another foray in search of material. She had heard the thumping of his heavy hiking boots, and when he had come into the kitchen for breakfast, dragging his pack like a reluctant dog behind him, she had been unwise enough to complain at being left alone again.

A grin had spread across his rugged features. 'Why? Will you miss me?' He'd taken a hunk of cheese from the larder and put it in his pack.

'Not particularly,' she'd lied, spreading some of Mrs Talbot's jam on a slice of bread. 'Only you've got so many dirges already—you'll have to start thinking about a second volume at this rate.'

'Work too much for you?'

'On the contrary.' She'd screwed the lid back on the jam jar with unwarranted firmness. 'I've nearly finished that last batch of typing.' Then, to her dismay, she had heard herself say plaintively, 'Do you really have to go?' Shut *up*! she'd cautioned silently, you're sounding like a neglected wife.

He had positively preened with self-satisfaction. ''Fraid I do, Jess. This woman is supposed to have sheltered a young airman whose plane crashed during the war. I want to get the story as a link between pieces. Besides, I feel the need to live rough for a couple of days; you've been keeping me in the lap of luxury. I need to toughen up.'

This was a reference to a picnic Jess had organised the day before. She'd spread a cloth over a flat rock by the little stream she'd discovered, and in a fit of enthusiasm she'd gone so far as to put sprigs of oleanders in the water as decoration for the wine bottle cooling there. Andros had teased her about candelabra and damask napkins, but he had clearly enjoyed himself, and if she hadn't been so much on her guard she would have done, too.

In an effort to regain her detachment from him, she had looked round the kitchen walls and said determinedly, 'I think I'll give the walls a coat of whitewash when I've finished the typing, then. Cheer the place up.'

'Are you sure you want to, Jess? Why not wait till I get back?'

'No! I'll go and get the whitewash this morning. It shouldn't take too long.' She had tilted her chin as if daring him to disagree.

However, Andros had merely shrugged. 'If you insist. Far be it from me to discourage a willing slave. Oh, and when you're in Yerolimin collect the mail, will you?' He'd raised a mocking black brow. 'Maybe Kitty will have sent me a cheque and then you'll be free!' For so far there had been no word from Australia. Far from upsetting Jess, this taunt had helped to restore her aloofness from him, and shortly after he had left.

She quickly discovered that she'd been mistaken when she'd told Andros that whitewashing the kitchen wouldn't take long—something she could fit in between lunch and dinner!

First she had to thoroughly clean the high brick walls, and this was a full day's work. It was like cleaning under the sink again, but on a mammoth scale. She scrubbed, and threw out bucket after bucket of dirty water, occasionally cursing herself for offering to do this awful job in the first place, and more often cursing Andros for not being firmer and preventing her!

She spent a lot of time fixing a trestle for her bucket and brushes. It was a bit rickety, being a rough plank balanced between a flimsy ladder she had borrowed from the taverna and the step-ladder from the kitchen, but it worked. However, she was thankful when she'd done the upper part of the walls and ceiling and she could stand on the firm floor again.

It all took a great deal of backbreaking time, but at noon on the third day she only had about a square foot of wall down near the floor to do when she heard a car draw up outside. Then she heard the unmistakable sound of Andros's deep, slow voice. Her heart leapt, and in an effort to finish the little bit of wall that was left—so that he would get the full effect when he came in—she hastily thrust her brush into the bucket which was balanced on the trestle. It rocked dangerously, and then it slowly fell, tipping the entire contents on to her head.

Andros stood at the door. 'The walls would have been enough, Jess!' he said. To her consternation, a beautiful woman came and stood beside him. 'I've brought someone for lunch.' He turned to his exquisite companion. 'Gisele, may I present my girl Friday, Jessica Firbank. Jess, this is my friend Gisele von Durstein.'

The whitewash dropped down into a puddle at Jess's feet, coating her hair and shoulders and getting into her eyes. 'Lunch might take some time,' she said.

'We could eat out, Andros,' said the beautiful woman. She had a throaty voice with a slight German accent and, now that Jess had blinked most of the whitewash out of her eyes, she saw that she was not only extremely lovely, she was also perfectly groomed. From the top of her sleek red head to the tip of her scarlet-painted toes, she was immaculate. Her white linen slacks were spotless, and so was her navy silk shirt that was unbuttoned to show a generous amount of cleavage. Enormous sunglasses, rimmed in emerald plastic, were pushed up into her tidy bevelled hair, and when she lifted her hand to pull them down on to her nose several gold bracelets chinked softly. Everything about her was expensive, elegant, and chic. The antithesis of Jess standing dripping in her pool of white goo.

'I suggest you have a drink in the shade outside, Gisele,' Andros said, 'while I help Jess to clean up.'

'It would surely be easier for us to go to a restaurant,' the woman insisted. She did not acknowledge Jess. She behaved, in fact, as if Jess wasn't there.

'Why don't you do that, Andros?' Jess agreed. 'I can clean this up.'

'Don't be silly!' He put a bottle of ouzo and glasses on to a tray. 'You'll start drying soon, and then you'll go stiff. Your hair's going funny already.' He grinned as he ran cold water into a jug.

She put her hand up and her hair felt as if it was starched. 'Oh, lord!'

'Not to worry! It'll wash out.' He passed the tray to Gisele, who took it reluctantly. 'You just go and have a nice drink in the cool courtyard,' he told her. 'Jess will fix lunch as soon as we've cleaned up.'

'Really, darling! You are so stubborn,' Gisele protested, and the 'darling' cut through Jess like a knife.

'You know I want you to see the tower,' Andros said. 'Don't be difficult, there's a good girl.' He patted her familiarly on her trim *derrière* and Jess could have killed him.

Gisele bared her pearly teeth in a smile. She reminded Jess of a dangerous animal. 'For you, I will be good,' she fluted, retreating to the yard.

'It might be better if you took off with your...friend,' Jess suggested through lips that were stiffening rapidly.

'Now, don't *you* start! One difficult woman is all I can handle at a time.' He picked up the brush and wiped it over her shoulders before applying it to the bare spot on the wall. 'Waste not, want not,' he said cheerfully.

The floor cleaned off easily. More easily than Jess. She had to hold her head under the tap for a long time, while Andros scrubbed vigorously. It would have been fun if they'd been alone. They would have had a great old giggle. But the knowledge that Gisele was sitting waiting outside took away all pleasure.

'That will have to do for the time being,' Andros said, 'but you're still white in spots.'

'Thank you,' said Jess, wearily climbing to her room to change. Once there she defiantly put on a pair of ragged jeans and an old shirt, and yanked her wet hair back off her face with an elastic band. There didn't seem much point in trying to do much more with such powerful competition downstairs. And then she scolded herself for thinking like that. After all, she had spent six weeks discouraging Andros, she could hardly complain if he looked elsewhere for female companionship.

When she came down he had taken cheese and bread from the larder and was examining some rather tired-looking oranges. 'What can we rustle up for lunch?' he asked.

'There's a tin of ham—and tomatoes. I'll manage something.'

'Great!' He made for the low door, then turned. 'There's a bottle of red wine somewhere. Let's have that, too. Make it festive.'

As she opened tins, she thought bleakly that he seemed very anxious to impress. Clearly he wanted Gisele von Durstein to share his enthusiasm for his beloved Mani. Good luck! thought Jess grimly, for she didn't think that the sun-baked rocks in the heart of these cruel and marvellous mountains were the setting for an exotic creature like Gisele. Jess couldn't see her chipping away any of her long red nails to help Andros recreate his heritage.

She arranged a large tray with sliced ham, tomatoes, a basket of fresh bread and a dish of olives. At the back of a cupboard she found paper napkins, and she dumped these on the tray, together with two wineglasses. She just hoped he would appreciate the trouble she was going to for his fancy woman!

He got up from his chair when she came out with the tray. 'Idiot girl! Why didn't you call me?' he asked, taking the tray and putting it on the table.

'I was having too much fun carrying it myself,' she said. 'Besides, you're busy.' She looked over at Gisele, who was sipping ouzo delicately, and for a brief moment the two women appraised each other. It was only a momentary glance, but enough to establish the antagonism that had been hovering in the air like sea mist.

As she started to return indoors, Andros called, 'Why only two glasses? Aren't you having wine?'

'I've made a sandwich for myself,' she said from the doorway. I'll have it in my room.'

'Don't be bloody absurd!' he said. 'Get yourself a glass and bring your sandwich out here and join the party.'

She was going to refuse, when she saw Gisele's lips tighten. 'I'd love to,' Jess said then, and she thought, put that on your needles and knit it!

She fetched a glass and her plate, and sat facing them. Andros poured wine for them, cleared his throat for silence, and made a toast. 'To my two beautiful companions. The loveliest women in Greece.' His face was solemn, but his eyes sparkled with mischief. He was having a high old time, and Jess felt a surge of indignation at being teased like this. She took a large swallow of wine.

'Darling, you are so democratic,' purred Gisele, removing her sunglasses and arching her pencilled brows. She addressed herself to Jess for the first time. 'You are very fortunate to have such a democratic employer, Miss...er...'

'Oh, I *know*. He slums with the help all the time,' replied Jess, recklessly gulping her wine. 'Have you known each other long?' she enquired sweetly. 'Or did he pick you up today?' Andros chuckled and speared a piece of ham.

Gisele's green eyes narrowed. 'Our families have been friends for years,' she said coldly, 'but we met by chance yesterday. Andros was swimming in the sea like a...'

'Like a porpoise?' Jess cut in helpfully, holding out her glass for more wine.

'Like a handsome sea-god,' reproved Gisele.

Andros refilled Jess's glass and she looked at him a trifle muzzily. 'And what about the dirge lady?' she asked. 'Did you find her, or were you too busy playing sea-gods?'

'I found her *before* I took to the water,' he said, 'and I recorded a lot of material. You've got your work cut out for you.'

'Well, that should keep me out of mischief,' said Jess, sipping away. 'Not that there's much chance for mischief here, Miss von Durstein.' She looked pointedly at Andros. 'The possibilities are so limited.' She could feel the wine buzzing around in her head but she didn't care.

'Imagine my surprise,' Andros said chattily, 'when I swam up to this yacht and there was Gisele leaning over the rail.'

Gisele leaned towards him, showing a good deal of cleavage in the process. 'Like Penelope awaiting the return of Odysseus,' she murmured huskily.

'And there he was—flopping around in the water,' said Jess.

Andros smiled. 'I don't flop, actually,' he said. 'I'm quite a good swimmer.'

'Indeed you are,' said Gisele, turning her shoulder to Jess. 'You are magnificent in the water. The Baroness remarked on it.'

'But is he magnificent *out* of it?' asked Jess on the wings of her third glass of wine.

Gisele looked her full in the face. 'I can assure you that he *is*,' she said softly. She dismissed Jess and turned her full attention to Andros. 'Now, *liebling*, it is arranged that you will join us for a day soon. I am relying on it.' She put out her scarlet-tipped hand and squeezed his tenderly. 'As you have seen for yourself, there is plenty to do on board.'

'Yes, indeed!' He removed her hand in order to take an olive. 'I stayed on the yacht last night,' he said to Jess. 'It's quite a boat.'

That would explain his smooth-shaven chin, Jess thought resentfully. From the sound of it, this yacht was equipped with every convenience—including German mistresses.

'Toughening up, eh?' she said, and he grinned unrepentantly.

Gisele started talking to Andros about people Jess didn't know, so she chewed away at her sandwich, stoically telling herself that it was none of her business what had gone on on that yacht last night. It was none of her business if he and Gisele were lovers, it had nothing to do with her. Just the same, the food was tasteless in her mouth, and the wine was sour.

Meanwhile Gisele had started to nag, trying to fix exactly *when* Andros would join the party aboard the *Belle Hélène.*

'I must finish translating my notes first,' he said, and Jess was pleased to hear a note of irritation in his voice.

Gisele pushed aside her untouched plate of food. 'But when you have done that, *liebling,*' she said, 'I shall do all in my power to persuade you to spend the rest of the summer with us when we sail the Aegean Sea. Surely a cruise on the wine-dark sea of Greece is preferable to living in this stony place.'

'Cor, luv a duck!' muttered Jess into her wineglass. 'How about some coffee?' she said loudly when they both looked at her. She pushed her hair more tightly into its rubber band and discovered that it was stiff with whitewash, and she could feel that her cheeks were flushed with wine. Marvellous! She must look like some derelict he'd picked up off the Brighton beach.

'Coffee might be a good idea,' said Andros. He rose and offered his hand to the German woman. 'While you're getting it, I'll show Gisele over the tower.'

Jess watched them, as hand in hand they went through the low doorway, leaving her alone. She tipped the remaining food into the rubbish bin, too dispirited to save it. As she brewed coffee, she could hear Gisele's laugh and Andros's deep murmur, and she felt as lonely as if she were stranded on a desert island.

They returned long after she had taken the coffee tray out to the courtyard. This time Andros didn't protest when she said she would take hers up to her room. 'I'd have a nice rest, if I were you,' he said. 'You've earned it.'

'Yes.' She steeled herself to be polite. 'Goodbye, Miss von Durstein. I doubt we will meet again.'

'It is unlikely,' agreed Gisele haughtily.

The wine did its work and Jess slept heavily, waking at four with a headache. On her way downstairs she saw Andros in his office, working on his translations. There was nothing she could do yet, so she heated water and washed her hair and herself thoroughly, to remove all traces of her accident. Then she went for a walk to her shady oasis, where the oleanders grew. She patted her aching forehead with water from the icy steam and then looked down to where the ribbon of fertile earth petered out into rock again. Rock which fell in great sweeps to the sea.

This stony place, Gisele had called it. Well, she was right, it *was* that. A great carapace of limestone dotted with jungles of prickly pear, its villages bristling with towers—and already Jess loved it. In six short weeks it had captured her heart. Something in her psyche responded to its austere beauty, just as something she was unable to control responded to the man who had brought her here. She might fight him till she dropped, but something in her bones and blood told her that she would never be able to uproot him totally from her heart. Already he was as much a part of her as her flesh.

CHAPTER SIX

IT WAS sundown when Jess returned to the tower. Andros was already on the roof, a tray of drinks beside him. 'I was beginning to think you were lost,' he said. She smiled, but her heart called out, I am, dear God, I am!

'I'm glad you're here.' He smiled. 'I want to share the sunset with you. The sky's particularly lovely tonight.'

'Yes,' she agreed. But it was a little frightening too, blood-red and streaked with purple clouds that were lined with gold. And it was very still. There wasn't a breath of air, not even up on the tower. She helped herself to a glass of water. She couldn't face ouzo.

Andros looked at her keenly. His face was bronzed to an even darker shade so that his eyes seemed to glow. 'You're looking tired, Jess,' he said, tipping her chin gently with his long forefinger and tracing the shadows under her eyes with his thumb. She stood motionless under this caress, like a wild animal being gentled. 'We'll go out for dinner. No more cooking today. We'll go to Yerolimin. A reward for all your hard work while I was away. Would you like that?'

A reward for slaving away over the kitchen while he had fun with Gisele! She pulled her head back and said brusquely, 'Anything you like. You're the boss.'

'Yerolimin, then,' he said firmly. 'As soon as it's dark.'

She changed into a cool, full-skirted blue dress that was sprinkled with large white daisies, and Andros exchanged his disreputable shorts for white cotton trousers and a black shirt with the sleeves rolled high. His arms were the colour of teak and the disc of his gold watch gleamed like a sun on his sinewy wrist.

There was no moon and clouds hung low over the mountains. Even the breeze that blew in through the sunroof of the car was hot and gave no relief.

The taverna they chose at Yerolimin was full of people hoping to catch a breath of air from the sea. But even down by the quay the atmosphere was oppressive, as if the night was holding its breath. The water looked as heavy as oil under the lowering sky, and it swayed slightly with an uneasy motion that made Jess feel mildly seasick.

After he had ordered their dinner, Andros sat back with a cold beer while Jess sipped listlessly at a lemonade. 'Storm at sea,' he remarked, indicating the horizon and she saw a fork of lightning zigzag in the distance.

'I wish the storm *would* come,' he said. 'It rarely rains during the summer. The winter, now that's something else! My father told me that the wind used to whistle through the towers of Vathia like a wild beast.'

It was the first time he'd ever mentioned his family and Jess asked, 'Does your father live in England, too?'

Andros's expression became guarded. 'No. He... he died when I was sixteen.'

'I'm sorry, I didn't mean to pry.'

'You're not prying. My mother lives in England, in the country. She moved back to her home town when she was widowed.'

'To escape the winds of Vathia?' She smiled.

'Something like that. She never really took to Greece. She claims the winters in Athens were the coldest she'd ever known.'

'Sounds a bit like Brighton,' Jess observed.

'How long have you lived in Brighton?'

She wiped away the beads of moisture from her glass, tracing patterns on it with the tip of her finger. 'For about eighteen months. I moved there from Richmond where I worked in a dress shop... but you know all this, don't you?' she said remembering the enquiries he'd made.

'I only know the facts, not the personal reasons for all your moving about.'

Jess shrugged. 'Just general restlessness. I suppose I'm not a very stable person.'

'What rubbish!' He spoke with such force, her head jerked up. 'Oh, I admit that at first I might have agreed with you. But not now... not after living with you for six weeks.'

'That sounds a bit questionable,' she said.

However, Andros ignored her remark, and continued, '*Something* must be driving you. I'm curious.'

'Nothing's driving me,' she said testily, because he'd hit a nerve. 'I just moved away from the Midlands when my mother... went to live in America.'

'I didn't know your mother lived in the United States.' He moved the beer bottle to make room for a dish of *tzatziki* that the waiter put on the table.

'Mother lives in Wisconsin.' She took a spoonful of the yoghurt and cucumber salad on to her plate. Its pungent aroma, usually so appetising, made her feel rather sick. 'My stepfather's an American.'

'*Wicked* stepfather?' he asked quizzically.

'Not wicked at all. Rather a poppet, really... unlike Uncle Stanley.'

He paused in the act of dipping bread into his *tzatziki*. 'Uncle Stanley?'

'My first stepfather. He *wasn't* a poppet.'

'Do you collect them? Stepfathers. How many have you had?'

'Only two. Mum and Uncle Stanley divorced when I was twelve.' She pushed her plate aside. She was feeling decidedly unwell, and all this talk about her mother's matrimonial experiments wasn't helping.

But he went on prodding. 'What about your father? Did your mother divorce him, too?'

'No. He died when I was six. Mum married Uncle Stanley a year later.' She didn't say that if Colin Firbank hadn't died in a car crash it was pretty well on the cards that he and his young wife would have split up. Jess vividly remembered the quarrels between her parents. Her mother's tearful whine, and the slam of the front door when her father banged out of the house. That door had slammed more and more often during last days of her father's life.

The waiter brought a dish of baked red mullet, and Andros put some on to her plate. 'I didn't mean to upset you, Jess,' he said softly as he watched her push it half-heartedly around on her plate.

'I'm not upset,' she assured him, putting down her fork and eating a small piece of bread.

'Still, an unhappy childhood isn't very good dinner conversation,' he insisted.

'My childhood wasn't all unhappy. Fortunately, Uncle Stanley didn't like children, so I was sent to boarding-school the year they married.' He started to speak but she forestalled him. 'No, I *loved* it at school. When Mum took me out to live with her in Leicester, after the divorce, I nearly went into a decline.' She smiled wryly. 'Mum couldn't understand it.'

'So you went off on your own as soon as you could? To escape—er—family pressures?' She nodded. 'Life hasn't been awfully good to you, has it, Jess?' he said, his dark eyes soft as velvet.

Aghast, she felt the sting of tears. Self-pity was something she abhorred. She had witnessed too many glaring examples, what with her mother, and Aunt Mary, and now Kitty, to have patience with it. Under normal circumstances she wouldn't react to his kindness like this, but she wasn't well. In fact, she was becoming increasingly aware just how bad she was feeling. Her head had started to throb in earnest, and where she looked at Andros his craggy face wavered in a haze of pain.

'I'm...I'm feeling a bit dim tonight, Andros,' she said, putting a hand to her aching temple. Then she said, 'Oh dear!' because she suddenly knew she was going to be horribly sick. Leaping to her feet, she made a dash for the toilet.

Some minutes later she emerged, white and shaken. Andros was waiting near the door, and he came over to her and put his arm round her waist. She didn't try to push him away. Quite apart from the fact that she didn't want to, she wouldn't have had the strength. She leaned gratefully against his broad chest and let him take charge.

'Do you feel up to the drive home now?' he asked. 'Or would you like to sit quietly somewhere first?'

'Home,' she said, and that word sounded comforting. She smiled wanly at the restaurant owner who was hovering anxiously. 'Tell him that all I have is a migraine. It's nothing to do with his food.'

'He knows that,' Andros said. 'Stop worrying, love.' Then he took a firmer grip on her waist and half carried her out to the car.

'Hang on a minute,' he said when she was settled in her seat, and, going to the edge of the quay, he knelt down and dipped his handkerchief into the sea. 'Not very cold, I'm afraid.' Tenderly, he wiped her face.

'Thank you.' She would have loved to hold his hands against her cheeks while she sobbed her heart out, which was crazy because she wasn't unhappy. On the contrary, it was bliss having him taking care of her like this, and it was the feeling of being able to rely on someone else that made her feel weepy.

He drove carefully, avoiding the bumps in the road as much as he could, and taking the curves slowly. Once, to her mortification, they had to stop while she retired behind a large rock to be sick again. When the spasm had passed he helped her back to the car, and having him there, wiping her sweaty forehead, smoothing her tangled hair, wasn't humiliating at all. He didn't make a big production about it, but was sensible and sympathetic, and she allowed herself the comfort of leaning against him for the remainder of the journey.

By now the migraine had passed its climax, and although her head still ached abominably she didn't feel nauseous any longer. Back in the tower he told her to bathe her face while he put her mattress up on the roof. 'It'll be cooler up there,' he said. 'You'll sleep better.'

And when she had wearily climbed up the ladder she found that he'd made up her bed, and put a glass of cool water on the floor beside it.

He turned down the sheet. 'In you get.' Obediently, she did as she was told, not caring that she was clad in only a filmy nightie. He held out two aspirin tablets. 'Will these help?'

'I don't know... perhaps.' She swallowed them both with some of the water. She was feeling as dependent as a child, a sensation that was unfamiliar to Jess.

He smoothed her honey-gold hair from her brow. His hand felt nice and she gave a contented sigh. 'Will the light bother you?' He had put an oil lamp on the parapet.

'No. I hardly noticed it.'

'Then I'll sit and read for a bit. Just till you're settled. OK?'

'That would be nice,' she admitted drowsily.

As if in a dream, she felt his lips brush her eyelids and heard him whisper, 'Go to sleep... you're safe now, sweetheart.' And she gave a fluttering breath before falling into a dreamless sleep.

Once during the night she woke and, glancing over, saw him sitting, a massive silhouette in the soft lamplight. When she moved her head, he looked over to her.

'Go back to sleep, Jess,' he said softly, and she snuggled down happily, secure because he was near.

She woke to the sound of a cock crowing lustily somewhere in the village. For an instant she wondered who had played a practical joke by painting her ceiling to look like the sky; a sky that was pale green, edged with gold where the sun touched it. Then she remembered and looked over to where the lamp had been. It had gone, and there was no sign of Andros, either.

As always after a migraine, she felt particularly well. Leaping off her mattress, she energetically bundled the sheets together and returned to her room to dress. Her travelling clock showed that it was not yet six. She and that rooster seemed to be the only ones awake.

Creeping down to the kitchen, she passed through Andros's room. He was in bed and still asleep, the sheet draped over his body, one bare arm hugging the pillow.

She decided to bring his coffee up to him. It seemed the least she could do after his solicitude. While she spooned coffee into mugs and waited for the water to boil, she was conscious that every nerve in her body was tingling. She could still feel the light pressure of his lips on her eyelids and recall the feel of his gentle hand on her brow. It was as if, with his touch, her body had awakened and was now quivering with life, and her heart pounded painfully against her ribs when she climbed, carefully balancing the mug of Nescafé, to his bedroom.

He was still fast asleep, lying on his back now, his upper torso bare, the black hair on his chest crisply curling against his tanned skin. She put the coffee on the bedside table and looked down at him. His hair was a tousled blue-black cap of curls, and his eyelashes— she had never before realised what long eyelashes he had—were like a silk fringe.

This was the first time she had really lingered in Andros's bedroom. Even when she was in the tower alone, this room had seemed a dangerous place to be. His personality was so strong that she had the feeling he might be lurking somewhere in the shadows, and so she had always scurried through on her way to the office or to her own room. Even when she'd dusted and swept it she had hurried. Now she let her gaze wander over the big bed, the large painted wardrobe against one wall, his clothes dropped untidily on an upright chair of carved olive wood. On either side of the bed were matching bedside tables, painted iron stands topped with marble. A stack of books was on the one close to her, and she leaned forward to read their titles, her hair swinging loose on either side of her face.

A Greek/English dictionary, a detective novel, and a slim volume bound in plum-coloured suede. She picked up this last one. It looked new and smelt of perfume, and the suede felt smooth in her hand. It was a book of Elizabethan love poetry, printed on thick paper with rough edges, but it was the inscription on the fly-leaf that caught her eye. 'For Andros—To remind him,' it read, and the name that flowed boldly, right across the page, was 'Gisele'.

'Want to borrow it?' Andros's eyes were wide open.

She nearly dropped the book on the floor. 'Oh! I . . . I didn't know you were awake.'

He sat up in the bed, the sheet falling down to his hips, and now she saw that he was naked, his body strong and brown as a tree trunk.

'I—er—I brought you coffee,' she said, flustered.

'How nice.' He grinned and sat higher in the bed, the muscles on his shoulders gleaming in the growing morning light. 'Did you bring some for yourself, too?'

'No.' She backed away. 'Mine's in the kitchen.'

'How unfriendly. Why not bring it up here?'

'No, thanks. I've got things to do.'

He opened his black eyes in mock surprise. 'Not while you drink your coffee, surely?' Moving to the centre of the bed, he patted the edge invitingly. 'You won't have to sit on a hard chair.'

'I'd save that sort of invitation for...for someone else.' She scuttled over to the trapdoor. 'Don't flirt with me, Andros. I don't like it.'

'Consider it a waste of time, do you?' he enquired innocently. 'You the type who prefers to dispense with the preliminaries?'

'I'm the type who doesn't enjoy playing games with the boss.' She started backing down the ladder. 'I'm just an employee. I don't like to forget my place!'

It was a good thing, she thought as she went to the taverna to buy breakfast, it was a good thing she'd looked in that book and seen Gisele's signature, because if she hadn't she would certainly have ended up in bed with him. Fortunately, the memory of Gisele was a powerful brake on her desire. Jess was a proud lady, she didn't choose to play second fiddle—not even for a man as attractive as Andros.

He was washing at the kitchen sink when she returned, still stripped to the waist, but decently covered below now by his frayed shorts. Thinking about Gisele had made Jess feel so cross that she banged the frying pan about more than was necessary, and slapped the loaf of bread down on to the bread board quite violently.

'Headache gone, I presume?' he said, vigorously towelling his head.

'Quite gone, thank you.' She broke eggs into a bowl and beat them into a foam. 'Thank you for taking care of me last night. I'm sorry I was a bore.'

'You weren't a bore. You were rather sweet, actually.' He threw his towel up through the trapdoor to his room, and pulled on a red T-shirt. 'Too bad it takes a headache to sweeten you.'

She poured the egg mixture into the pan and started stirring. 'We can't help our natures,' she said, squinting up at him. 'You're not always sweetness and light yourself.'

'*Me!*' He looked outrageously innocent. The way he must have looked when he was a small boy caught in some devilment. 'I have the disposition of a *saint*! You should have heard my nanny on the subject.'

'You probably bribed her with your pocket money,' said Jess, but she smiled, because when he was in this charming jokey mood she found it impossible to stay angry. By the time she'd eaten her second helping of scrambled eggs—she was always ravenous after a migraine—they were laughing together again.

The morning passed slowly. Jess typed up the translations Andros had completed, and then wrote a long letter to her mother. She had already told Angela that she had a secretarial job in Greece for the summer, but she had not been surprised when her mother had not referred to it. Angela never referred to things that were not directly related to her. In fact, her last letter had been one long moan about the difficulty of living in America, the problems of dealing with her husband's relatives, and the general disappointment she felt about life.

Jess ignored these complaints and wrote describing the Maniot landscape, her work on the dirges, and the general atmosphere of the place, although she knew it was really a waste of time. Angela would merely skim through it and then sit down and write another long litany about her failed dreams.

When she had finished, she sent her love to her stepfather. In the past she had always included a separate note for him, but she'd stopped doing this since Angela's letters had become so bitter. She didn't want to take sides in what was clearly an on-going domestic squabble, and she knew her mother would view any enclosures as a betrayal of faith on Jess's part. It was a difficult situation, and as far as Jess was concerned yet another indication of the pitfalls that accompanied matrimony.

Before noon, Andros came into the office with a folder of translations, but when she took the cover off the typewriter he put it back on again.

'Oh, no! I'm declaring the rest of today a holiday.' She opened her mouth to protest, but he laid two fingers over her lips. 'A *holiday*! I'm the boss—remember?'

'Very well.' Oh, God! How she'd wanted to kiss those restraining fingers...bite them erotically...

'Let's go to Yerolimin and put together a picnic,' he said, half lifting, half dragging her from her chair. 'I know a nice beach we could siesta on. Great swimming— how about it?'

She was reluctant because the thought of being alone on a beach with Andros, both of them barely clothed, seemed more temptation than she could cope with, but he overrode her.

'Come on!' he insisted. 'It's hot, and by this afternoon it'll be like an oven.' She agreed then, for the thought of swimming in cool water was irresistible.

Once in town, Andros left her sitting under the awning of a taverna while he shopped for food. 'You sit still and take it easy,' he said, 'to make up for last night.'

She sipped the cold lemonade he'd ordered and looked out from under the brim of her straw hat at the little boats bobbing up and down at their moorings. The sea glittered like mica in the noonday sun. A fisherman skilfully mended a net, deftly twisting the twine in his horny fingers, as dexterous at the work as his wife was at her weaving loom. How lovely it was here, Jess thought, leaning further back in her chair and letting the sounds of the sleepy little town drift over her. If only she had been visiting under different circumstances. If she and Andros had met by chance here...and there had been no Gisele...

She stopped lounging and sat up straight. No good living in a dream world. She could either settle for a summer of hard work, grateful that she'd been shaken out of her rut and given a chance to earn a lot of money, or she could stop dithering like a Victorian spinster and have a fling with her employer—Gisele or no Gisele. But she wasn't able to do that. So stop mooning! she told herself sternly, you're a big girl and you must look out for yourself! And, when Andros joined her, her back was rigid and her lips were folded tight. Every guard up to protect herself against him.

He dropped some letters in front of her. 'Here's your share. Now, how about another lemonade before we head off for the beach?'

'Not for me, thank you.' She sounded as distant as if she was sitting on another planet, but she didn't care. She wanted to keep a gulf between them, it was her only safety. She reached for her letters. 'Would you excuse me if I just glance at these?'

'I wonder you can do it without white gloves on,' he drawled, pulling a sheaf of envelopes out of his briefcase. 'Anyway, *I'm* going to have a coffee while I go through this lot.'

Jess's mail was not particularly interesting. Some forwarded bills, a note from Tony, and a short letter from Mrs Talbot telling her that the weather had been 'a right scandal' in Brighton, and to 'hurry up and come back soon because they missed her something shocking'. There was no word from Kitty.

'Did you bring sunglasses?' asked Andros.

She came to with a start. 'Pardon?'

'Sunglasses. Did you bring some? You'll need them on the beach as well as that fetching hat,' he smiled genially.

'I have some in my bag.' Better keep this businesslike, she thought, so she added, 'I brought my shorthand pad, too. In case you want to dictate some letters.'

'On a hot afternoon on the beach? What a grisly notion!'

'Well, I am here to work, after all.' Her mouth set primly. 'I'm not here to loll about on beaches.'

'I've never seen anything less like lolling than you,' he grumbled. 'Look at you! Sitting up as if you were

still solidified in whitewash.' He leant across the table
and put his hand on hers. 'I give you full permission to
enjoy yourself, Jessica. I think we would both have a
rewarding time if you did.'

'If you want a playmate, I suggest you give—someone
else a call,' she said, disengaging her hand. 'Don't forget
I'm just an employee.'

'How *can* I forget it when you mention it every five
minutes? So I'm firing you.' And when she gasped he
added, 'For today. You go back on the payroll tomorrow.
All right?' And Jess laughed shakily and shrugged her
slender shoulders.

The beach Andros drove them to was only a kilometre
or so from Vathia: a small crescent of polished pebbles
and white sand rimmed with water so clear and blue that
it looked unreal. After they had clambered down the
rocky goat track, Andros pulled off his shorts. Under
them he was wearing a pair of white bathing trunks. The
black hair on his chest thinned to a V over his hard flat
stomach, the muscles on his strong thighs rippled. He
looked like a Greek statue come to life.

Jess was also wearing her bathing suit under her
clothes, and as she pulled her dress over her head she
was conscious that he was watching her closely. She suddenly felt very naked, for this particular swimsuit, an
emerald green bikini, was merely two triangles tied with
strings over her hips, and two even smaller triangles over
her ripe young breasts.

He spread two towels out in the shadow cast by the
cliff and effortlessly sat down on one of them.

'Oh, it is nice and cool here,' she said, starting to
babble. 'Shall we swim first? Or have our lunch? I don't
really believe that you sink like a stone if you swim too
soon after eating, do you?'

He smiled, a loving, gentle smile that turned her limbs
to water. 'You can do whatever you want, Jess. You
choose.'

'Oh! Well...maybe we should eat.'

He reached up and pulled her down gently, so that she was sitting on the towel beside him.

'You are a funny girl,' he said. He still held her hand and now he lightly stroked the inside of her wrist with his thumb. She had about as much resistance to this caress as wax to the sun. 'One minute you're warm and friendly, and the next you're as spiky as the prickly pears that grow around the tower. And you're so tense...'

She wondered if he could feel her pulse fluttering under his touch. That undisciplined pulse of hers, that betrayed her so completely.

'Let's just have a nice lazy time together...as friends.' His thumb was still hypnotically stroking her wrist, sending all kinds of delicious sensations through her. She wanted to slide down on to her back and pull him on top of her. Feel his heavy weight on her—his mouth roaming over her body...

She made a gigantic effort of will, removed her hand, and said in a croak, 'I'm *starving*! Let's eat, shall we?'

His lips twisted into a wry grimace. 'She'd rather eat than anything else!' he mocked. Briefly cupping her face in his hands, he said, 'Don't look so worried, Jess. Relax! This is a holiday...remember?'

'It takes me a while to get into a holiday mood,' she told him, starting to unwrap the food.

Andros had bought a delicious lunch. A carton of freshly cooked shrimp, and another of cucumber salad with olives, eggs, and radishes from the taverna. Bread, various cheeses, and little melons the size of cricket balls, that were full of juice and sweet as honey. He'd brought wine, too, which he lay in the wet sand to cool.

'What a feast!' she cried as she unpacked a lump of *halva*, that luscious Greek sweetmeat made of ground almonds. 'And proper wineglasses, too! Andros, how classy!'

'You're a very classy lady,' he said, and his voice held such promise that all her warning signals went off simultaneously and she jumped to her feet.

'You know, I think I *will* have a swim first,' she cried, running as fast as she could into the translucent water that was so blue it was like running into the heart of a sapphire. She swam out quite far, until she could see the top of the cliffs.

Andros watched her for a little while, and then he too walked into the sea and swam towards her, his powerful body cutting through the water with scarcely a ripple. When he reached her, he said, 'What a marvellous swimmer you are. Like a seal.'

'You could have said a mermaid. Seals don't have very pretty figures,' she said, and realised that it was an idiotic thing to say if she wanted to keep him at arm's length.

'This one does,' he said. His hair was slicked back from his broad forehead, and his muscular body, clearly visible in the crystal water, was burnished to an even darker brown by the sea.

Jess trod water, splashing more than was necessary. 'What a marvellous spot!'

'It's particularly marvellous *now*,' he replied, and she looked at him earnestly, her grey eyes wide. 'Come on!' he said, 'I'll race you back to shore. I'll count to twenty to give you a head start.'

She laughed then. 'Conceited ass!' And, turning in the buoyant water, she struck out for the shore.

She was in shallow water when he caught up with her. 'Got you!' He grabbed her by her long golden legs and pulled her under.

She surfaced, spluttering and laughing. 'Not fair! I would have won. Most un-English behaviour!' She splashed water at him and he took her by the shoulders and held her close. She could just touch the sandy bottom.

'All's fair in love and war,' he said huskily, then he bent over and kissed her on the lips. The hairs of his moustache brushed her soft mouth, and a tingle of pleasure travelled through her body.

He lifted her up out of the water, and held her tightly against him, so that her breasts were crushed against his chest. His skin felt cool against hers. To keep her balance she was forced to wind her arms round his neck, and his kiss grew deeper. She wanted to lose herself, to surrender to the pleasure of his darting tongue, without thought for anything else.

Andros released her mouth at last and brushed her neck and shoulders with his lips, biting gently on her earlobe. Then he licked her and, involuntarily, she shivered with delight.

'You're all salty,' he said, and his usually gentle voice was rough. 'Like a sea-goddess.'

He took her hand and led her out of the water, and Jess clung to him because her legs felt weak. When they reached the cliff, he picked up one of the towels and wrapped her in it, then he held her close again. She could feel the hardness of his body pressed against hers. Hard chest and thighs. A man's hardness.

'Why don't you take off that wet suit?' he said unevenly, rubbing his hand up her back under the towel until his fingers found the tie of her bra, which he undid. 'Let me help you.'

'No!' She stepped back as the flimsy bikini top slid to the sand. 'No...please.' She clutched at the towel.

Thoughtfully he said, 'Perhaps you're right. Perhaps this isn't the place.' And, reaching out, he tucked a strand of her wet hair behind her ear. 'I'm going to have another swim, then we'll have lunch.' He smiled then, and his mouth was tender. 'There's nothing to worry about, Jess. I promise you.'

It was all very well for him to say that, she thought, as he swam away. As far as she could see, there was *everything* to worry about! She secured her bra-strings firmly. Here she was, miles from anywhere, and all he had to do was reach out and touch some part of her anatomy and she was reduced to jelly. She had never reacted to a man's touch like this before. *Never!* She would really have to get a grip on herself, otherwise, before she knew it, she'd be in trouble . . . or in his arms, which amounted to the same thing.

She moved her towel about six feet away from his and settled down to comb out her damp hair. The important thing was not to lose her head. The next time he tried to make love to her—for he certainly would try again— she must not allow herself to be trapped by her body's response. She *must* remain in control.

This, she knew, was easier said than done, but she had to try, and when Andros came dripping out of the water, like Poseidon, god of the sea, and sat down near her, she managed to continue to braid her hair with a steady hand.

They ate lunch and spent the rest of the afternoon dozing, swimming at intervals, and reading. Andros didn't try to kiss her, or even touch her, except in the most casual way, and this helped. It also, paradoxically, disappointed her a bit.

When the sun was turning the colour of old gold and the little beach was all in shadow, they packed up for home. The water was grape-coloured now, and the air refreshing, but the tension between them started to build again, to seethe with an erotic vitality, so that by the time they were back in the tower her heart was beating thickly with anticipation. When she had changed into a clean dress she came down to find Andros sorting out the remains of their picnic.

'I don't know about you,' he said, 'but I'm not hungry enough for dinner. How would it be if we simply finished the remains of lunch?'

'That would be fine by me.' She doubted she'd be able to swallow a bite, anyway, she was so nervous. 'Shall we have it on the roof?'

'I've got a better idea.' His eyes looked like black agate in the dim lamplight. 'Why don't we go to that little stream? It's such a lovely night.' He held up the winebottle. 'Look! We've even got some wine left.'

'I don't know...' Drinking wine in the moonlight didn't sound a very safe plan. But neither did being alone with him in the tower...or on the roof, so she agreed.

'Good girl!' He re-packed their meagre supper, took two fresh wineglasses from the cupboard, and they set off.

The moon was so bright that the towers shone as if they were wrapped in silver paper. Each stone on the path ahead cast an individual shadow, as black and distinct as if drawn in Indian ink. They could see the little puffs of dust that flew up from under their sandals as they wound their way up towards the little natural garden in the barren rock.

Moonlight had bleached the colour from the oleanders, and the undersides of the plane tree's leaves were like cloth of silver. The only sound in the stillness was the trickle of the tiny waterfall as it spilled into its pool. He put the basket down and looked around this tiny oasis. 'This was a good idea,' he said, smiling down at her.

'It certainly is a nice spot.' Be obvious, be boring, she urged herself, then maybe he'll lose interest.

He stroked her cheek. 'It's cool and fresh and lovely. Just like you.'

She gave a nervous little laugh, for in spite of all her discipline his touch still made her tremble.

He lay the bottle in the rocky basin while she put the checked cloth over a flat rock and unpacked the food. It was simple. Cheese, fruit, and what was left of that morning's bread.

He went to put his arm round her shoulder, but she broke free, crying shrilly, 'I'm *dying* for a glass of wine. Let's not wait for it to cool.'

Andros poured them both a glass, then sat on the ledge of rock, pulling her down beside him. 'To you,' he said softly. 'You are as beautiful as the moonlight, and as surprising as...'

'As what?' she choked.

He put his glass down and pushed his hands into her hair, which was loose over her shoulders, lifting the weighty mass and letting it spill through his fingers. 'As surprising as a nereid,' he whispered.

Curiosity got the better of her and she asked, 'What *is* a nereid, exactly?'

'Nereids are spirits from the ancient world. They haunt remote streams and are beautiful...' he took the glass from her unresisting fingers and put it down '...and wanton.'

His lips were firm, and the taste of him was better than wine, but she broke away and, with a shaky laugh, said, 'Would you like some cheese?'

He lifted her to her feet and, taking her in his arms, said gruffly, 'I don't want any damn cheese. I want *you*!'

'Please, Andros!' She pushed at his chest, but he simply buried his face in her mass of shining hair and said, 'Oh, God, you're so beautiful!' He kissed her lips urgently, and she sighed and trembled. 'We're so good together,' he whispered. 'Don't fight me off.' He nuzzled the warm curve of her neck. 'Let's make this a summer to remember.'

A summer to remember. It would be that, all right! And afterwards? Would those memories keep her warm during the long English winters? Because she *would* remember him. All her life. He wasn't the sort of man a girl forgot in a hurry. And she mustn't, *couldn't*, let that happen. She couldn't afford that kind of pain.

She avoided his searching lips, pulling herself away from him. 'A summer fling?' she asked. The moonlight made her eyes shine. 'With no strings attached?'

He looked at her enigmatically. 'Not a single string, if that's the way you want it.' Reaching out, he caught her chin and held it so she was forced to look into his face. 'And that *is* the way you want it, isn't it, Jess?'

'Not with you,' she said, and that was the truth. A casual affair, with no strings attached, was the last thing she wanted with him.

His face became flint hard and he let go of her chin. 'Of course,' he said, 'I forgot. I'm not your type, am I?'

'Not remotely, I'm afraid.'

'You bloody little liar,' he snarled. Swiftly, he touched her breast and pinched her diamond-hard nipple. 'You want me to make love to you. You're longing for it. Your body doesn't lie, even if you do.'

'I can't help my animal reactions,' she said fiercely, glad that he had touched her in that insolent way, for it had sparked her temper, and as long as she was angry she could keep desire at bay. 'I'll thank you to keep your hands to yourself in future.'

He leaned towards her, his face twisted with rage. 'Stop talking like a common tart,' he hissed, and this unexpected slap of rudeness made her gasp. 'I've never forced myself on a woman, and I don't intend to start now. You're quite safe.'

'Good!' she quavered idiotically.

'In fact, you needn't bother to put those cannon balls on your trapdoor any more,' he went on furiously. 'I might have been tempted before, but now I wouldn't touch you if you *begged* me.'

'I just want you to leave me alone, that's all,' she said, fighting to keep the tears out of her voice.

'I can promise you I'll do that,' he rasped. 'You may be a desirable woman, but if there's one thing I can't stand it's a phoney.'

She said flatly, 'That's that, then,' and in the ensuing silence half-heartedly started rewrapping the food.

He picked up their glasses and was about to put them back in the basket when, with a violent curse, he flung them against the rocks, where they shattered to fragments, and with one last furious glare he strode off, back to the silent village of towers.

CHAPTER SEVEN

VERY carefully, Jess picked up the shards of glass and dropped them down a crevice in the rocks. She was so numb, it was hard to make her fingers work properly. She concentrated carefully on repacking the food, slowly folding the paper napkins and putting each item back in the basket, as if neatness was a matter of the utmost importance. On the road below, headlights beamed across the chaos of rock, and she heard the distant roar of a speeding car. It was the first time she'd heard a car at night in these parts, and she was pretty sure it was Andros, getting as far away from her as he could. Her eyes filled with tears so that the oleander bushes and the plane trees slid together in a blur. Hastily, she blinked them away. No point in crying over spilt milk. She had wanted to discourage him, and now she had achieved that end, so why be so dreadfully upset?

Because she would almost certainly have to leave now. Leave Andros. And it was this thought that kept her blinking away tears as she picked her way down the path to the village.

The tower was in darkness when she got back and, sure enough, Andros's car was gone. With a heart like lead, Jess crawled up to her room to bed, taking a glass of wine with her for consolation, and poor consolation it was, too! She still put the cannon balls on her trapdoor. Not that she imagined she needed protection, but because it comforted her to see them there.

She was tired, but she didn't fall asleep for a long time, and when she woke at dawn her heart felt as heavy as the cannon balls. As she pulled on her jeans, she saw

117

from one of the narrow windows that Andros's car was parked again behind the tower, and this made her fingers all thumbs as she struggled with the buttons of her shirt.

She crept downstairs, praying she wouldn't wake him when she went through his room. She needed a strong cup of coffee before she encountered him. But she need not have worried, his bed was empty and had clearly not been slept in.

Downstairs, she made coffee and set the table for breakfast. She was shaking, for she dreaded the coming interview, when she would have to tell him that of course she would leave Vathia now. The fact that she suspected he would want her off the premises as soon as possible did nothing to cheer her up.

When Andros did come in he barely acknowledged her. He sat at the table gulping black coffee, not touching the bread and honey she had put out. He was unshaven and his face was drawn. The two lines that bracketed his mouth looked as if they had been freshly chiselled, they were so deep. She poured him a second cup of coffee without being asked.

'Andros,' she wrenched out finally, 'I realise, of course, that I can't... can't go on working for you...' He looked at her directly for the first time. His eyes were bloodshot, and in spite of her misery she attempted a feeble joke. 'You look the way I feel,' she said, but there was no answering glint in his eyes.

'What the hell are you talking about?' he asked roughly.

'About leaving...being fired...going home.' Her voice wobbled dangerously.

He looked at her acrimoniously. 'You're not going anywhere. Not until I hear from your cousin. We made a bargain, remember?'

'Yes, but...'

'Don't argue. You're my collateral.'

'Yes,, but...after last night...' Faint wings of hope had started to flutter in her breast. Maybe she *could* stay with him, after all!

He squinted at her sourly. 'Forget about last night. I have.'

Like hell you have, thought Jess happily. 'I just thought it might be awkward around each other now,' she insisted, hoping to force him to say that he wanted her to stay.

But all he said was, 'It won't be awkward around me, because I'll be away most of the time.'

She stretched out her long legs and stared at the tips of her sandals. 'I won't have much to keep me busy,' she murmured pensively. 'Maybe I could take a small trip, on one of my days off. There's a ferry to Crete from one of the ports, isn't there?'

His face darkened with fury and for a moment she thought he might hit her.

'I'm not giving you time off to traipse over to Crete and visit your tame archaeologist,' he snarled. 'I'll find enough work for you.'

She'd completely forgotten about her plane companion. Apparently Andros hadn't! She straightened in her chair. 'It was just a thought.' She started clearing the table. 'Now I'd better get on with those translations.'

'Leave them,' he said harshly. 'Today I'm going to Cape Matapan—and you're coming with me.'

She knew about Cape Matapan. The southernmost tip of the Deep Mani. A bony finger of rock pointing into the sea. Barren, inhospitable, and steeped in legend. 'Afraid I might run away to Crete?' she enquired innocently. 'Want to keep an eye on me, do you?'

He refused to enter into her banter. 'Don't be damn silly,' he growled. 'Get a move on, or it'll be noon before we get out of here.'

As she packed food, Jess told herself that his male pride had been wounded, and it took more than a few hours for male pride to recover, so she would have to be patient. Nevertheless, she didn't feel enthusiastic about this trip. She felt even less so after she had called up to the office to ask whether they should take lemonade or water to drink.

'*Water!*' he bellowed back. 'This isn't one of your cosy picnics, this is hot slogging. Lemonade will just make us thirstier.' Boy, oh, boy! she said to herself as she ran water into the flasks, this is going to be one heck of a day!

A short while later they were ready to start. It was hard to believe that Andros was in reality a civilised London businessman. Wearing jeans and hiking boots, a stained and weathered hat jammed on his head, he bore a closer resemblance to his tough Maniot past than to his urbane English present.

Since she didn't have walking boots, Jess was forced to settle for sneakers, and she also wore her wide-brimmed straw hat. It looked rather at odds with a plaid shirt and jeans, but it would protect her from the fierce sun, for even in the *shade* the Peloponnese sun could give one a sunburn.

They drove along an unfamiliar road to the eastern shore. Here the land narrowed to a saddle with a deep bay scooped out on either side, as if a giant had taken a bite out of both sides of a slice of bread. Soon the road stopped and turned into a goat track that clung perilously to one side of the steep cliff. Andros parked the car and reached for the backpack. 'From here, we walk,' he informed her.

'I rather gathered that.' She peered down the vertiginous slope, at the bottom of which lay the sea, vivid green and frilled with foam where it pounded against the base of the cliff. The landscape was without colour apart from that strip of brilliant water.

'Come on!' he shouted. 'Stop gawking! We're not on a sightseeing expedition!'

For some time after that they didn't speak. Not that Jess would have had the energy for conversation, even if she'd felt like it. It was now ten by her watch, and already the heat was intense. Once they had started their descent, what little breeze there was on top of the cliff was gone. Her shirt was sticking to her back, and she could feel the beads of moisture trickling from her forehead, but was unable to wipe her face for she needed both hands to cling to the sparse vegetation that dotted the edge of the path. Her sneakers slipped all the time on the loose stones and she kept losing her balance. It was only her determination not to show any signs of weakness that kept her on her feet at all.

Finally, Andros called a halt for a short rest and a drink of water. Jess didn't even bother to look for a comfortable place to sit, but fell on to the path, sure that she would never be able to rise again. He passed her the flask first and she took a gulp. It was like nectar, and she took another deep draught. 'You shouldn't drink so fast,' he nagged, 'just moisten your lips at first and then sip. Otherwise you'll get sick, and then you'll be worse than useless.'

'Sorry,' she replied meekly, although she felt like bashing him with the flask. 'Might I ask what it is we're looking for, or are we merely here for the sake of exercise?'

'There's a legend that says there are caves on the side of this cliff,' he said. 'Caves where the old Maniot pirates hid their treasure.'

'We're on a treasure hunt, then?' She tried a winsome smile which was a dismal failure.

'They blocked the caves with stones,' he said shortly, 'but there is a story in the family that one of my ancestors...'

'One of the *pirates*?' she prompted.

'One of my *ancestors* hid his treasure there. I thought it would be fun to see for myself.'

'*Enormous* fun!' She examined her heel, where a blister was forming. 'And when we've found this cave, what do we do? Dig with our bare hands?'

'I take a photo of it for my book,' he indicated the camera round his neck, 'and we go back to Vathia.'

'Are there no postcards of these caves?' There was an edge to her voice, but he ignored it and, putting the flask back, he pulled himself to his feet.

'Come on! We might as well get as far down as we can before it gets too hot.'

Why don't we just *roll* down?' she muttered under her breath. 'It couldn't be worse than walking.'

It was like climbing down a cliff in Hades with the devil leading, for by now if Andros had sprouted horns and cloven hooves she wouldn't have been surprised. Only a devil could be impervious to this glaring sun, this suffocating heat and punishing track. It wouldn't have surprised her, either, if the rocks had cracked in the fierce sunshine that burned with a relentless white light. She had rolled her sleeves down to protect her arms, but she could feel her ankles, between the cuffs of her jeans and her sneakers, turning red with sunburn. She stopped several times to apply sun-block to her tender skin, not caring now if she kept up with her tormentor or not. She almost wished she *would* keel over with sunstroke and crash to the rocks below—it would serve him right!

At last the path made a sharp turn, and a depression in the side of the cliff offered a little shade. By the time she staggered down to it Andros was sitting there, unpacking the food for their lunch.

'We'll stop here until the sun goes to the other side,' he looked at his watch, a sturdy waterproof one today, 'which should be in about two hours.'

'You mean, we get time to rest? Isn't that rather self-indulgent?' she said, collapsing on to the ground with a groan.

He continued unpacking the backpack. His face was streaked with dirt and sweat and the blue stubble on his chin made him look untamed. For a moment she had wild fear that he planned to do something dreadful. Rape her, or leave her alone to find her own way out of this barren hell as punishment.

However this terrifying thought vanished when he said quite kindly, 'I didn't know it was such a climb or I'd never have asked you to come.'

She reached for the water-flask and took a sip before saying, 'You mean, I've been sufficiently punished for last night?'

His brows drew together in a straight line. 'I admit I wanted to punish you,' he said gruffly, and picking up one of the many stones that lay around them he examined it closely before slinging it over the cliff edge. It glinted in an arc before falling out of sight. 'Male pride is notably sensitive—and Greek male pride is particularly so. My pride is one of my worst faults. That . . . and a hideous temper. I apologise.'

She stared at him in disbelief. *Andros! Apologising?* How absolutely incredible! Her resentment disappeared like magic, but all she said in a precise little voice was, 'Let's forget it, shall we?'

'We can try.' He looked at her keenly, and his heart contracted because she looked so fragile, with her ankles smeared with white cream, and that ridiculous hat tied under her chin, making her look like a schoolgirl.

'Now,' she said, 'what did I bring to eat?' She rummaged among the containers she'd packed, but her fatigue had miraculously diminished. This awful climb felt like a shared adventure now, rather than a solitary penance. 'That's quite a view!' She nodded happily at the cliffs. They were two thirds of the way down, and the sea shimmered below them like tumbled pale green silk. The noon light, which was more silver than gold, gilded the austere landscape like a giant spotlight, and the sky seemed higher and vaster than any sky she had ever seen before.

Andros cracked and peeled a hard-boiled egg. 'It should only take me about fifteen minutes to get down to where the caves are supposed to be,' he said. 'There's no need for you to come. I only need a couple of photos. It won't take long.'

She was going to say that, having come this far, she might as well go the whole way, but then she thought better of it. It was pleasant here in the shade, and caves were not one of her favourite things. 'Will you go as soon as we've finished lunch?'

'I guess so.' He gave her a tentative smile. 'Later on, we could find a taverna and have a meal on the way back. How does that sound?'

'It sounds great.' She leaned back against the rock, glad that they were friends again, although that crackle of sexuality was back. To be honest, it had never really disappeared, for no matter how angry she might be with him she still found him overpoweringly attractive. Back to square one! she mused wryly, stretching out in her corner of shade and pulling her hat down over her face.

'Here!' He leant over her and she could smell his skin, feel the warmth of him as he pushed the pack under her head. 'It makes quite a good pillow. I don't need it now.'

'Th-thanks!' It took all her will-power not to pull his head down on her breast and plunge her fingers into his tangle of dark curls.

'I'm off, then,' he said. 'I won't be long. A couple of hours, at most.'

'Be careful,' Jess told him, settling herself into a more comfortable position as she watched him striding down the cliffside. Then she sighed contentedly and soon drifted into a deep sleep, for she was very tired after all that exercise in the sun.

She awakened suddenly to a shower of pebbles and the clank of bells. Sitting bolt upright in a panic, at first she didn't remember where she was, then the sight of the bare cliffs and the muted sound of surf reminded her.

A flock of half-wild goats was what had awakened her. They only stayed long enough to gaze at her briefly through their flecked yellow eyes before turning and scampering away, their hooves sending a shower of stones and dust into the air.

The side of the cliff was completely in the shade now, and the silver light had turned to gold. Looking at her watch, Jess saw that it was nearly five-thirty. *Five-thirty!* That meant Andros had been gone nearly four hours! Hastily climbing to her feet, she wondered where on earth he could be, and fear clutched at her throat, for if he had fallen into the sea he would have been battered against the rocks. There was no chance of swimming in that turbulence. Firmly she banished this nightmare and, cupping her hands, she yelled his name as loudly as she could. Her voice echoed on the evening air. She picked up their things and, thrusting them into the pack, started off down the cliff, pulling it on to her shoulders as she went. The muscles of her calves felt sore, but she ignored this and, falling and sliding, she ran as fast as she could down the rutted path.

Near the base of the cliff she could see the outline of caves, most of them filled with rocks. Her heart sank. There must have been about a dozen of these openings, some completely choked with boulders, some with a fissure wide enough to admit a man. Which one would Andros have chosen?

She went to the nearest and squeezed in. A flurry of swallows whose nests were clinging to the cave walls flew out, making her jump. *'Andros, Andros!'* she called, and from the blackness her voice echoed back mockingly, 'Annndross!'

She tried two more caves with no success. There must have been a spectacular sunset round the western side of the Mani, for the sea was the colour of gold mixed with blood, but sunsets meant that it would be dark soon, and Jess had to bite on her lips to stop herself from sobbing with panic.

She climbed into a large cave that was partially hidden by a bush of prickly pear which tore at her clothes and scratched her face. *'Andros!'* she called again, and then her heart gave a great leap, for she heard his voice coming faintly from the interior.

'Here! I'm down here, Jess! I'm further in. Do you have the pack?' he called.

'Yes.'

'There's a torch in it. If you use that, you'll find me. I'm just down a bit and to your right.'

With hasty fingers, she fumbled in the backpack and found a heavy waterproof torch. She switched it on and played the beam on the walls of the cave. A couple of bats, disturbed by the light, flew out towards the opening and she gasped with alarm.

'I'm not far away,' he called. 'First turning on your right, about twenty yards from the entrance.'

She stumbled down the cave, which opened out to a wide hall with several openings running down from it and, taking the one to her right, she walked down it for several yards, then she almost fell over Andros, who seemed to be sitting on a ledge.

'Am I glad to see you!' he said.

'Are you hurt?' She reached for his hand, wanting to reassure herself that he was real, that this wasn't some cruel mirage fate had conjured to torture her with.

'I don't think so. My foot's stuck in this damn crevice and I can't get it out. I can't move the boulder.'

She shone the torch down and saw that his right foot was wedged in a crack between two large rocks. She pushed hard against the smaller one, but it was much too heavy for her to move.

'You'll never budge it,' said Andros. 'It needs a crowbar and at least two men. You'll have to go for help.'

'Yes.' Where on earth would she find help in this out-of-the-way spot?'

He reached into his trouser pocket. 'Here are the car keys. And take the torch. Could you leave the pack with me? There are a couple of candles in it and some matches.'

Fear gave way to anger, and in her relief she exploded, 'You idiot! You stupid...*stupid*... What on earth do you mean, exploring caves without a light?'

'I did have a torch,' he soothed. 'A little one.' He held up a pocket torch. 'It gave up the ghost about an hour ago. But you're quite right, I *was* careless.' He gave a faint grin. 'Too much *raki* last night. My mind hasn't been functioning right all day.'

'You *fool*!' She gave a choked sob.

'And what took *you* so long, if it comes to that?' he asked. 'I thought you'd decided to abandon me.'

'I slept until some goats woke me.' She gave a little gulp. 'I might have been asleep still if they hadn't.'

His teeth gleamed in the gloom. 'We're a great pair. You sleep like a dormouse, and I fall down holes!'

'I believe it's called adventure,' she said shakily.

'*Misadventure,* you mean! But it could be worse, Jess.'

She put her hand on his shoulder. She had to keep touching him, feel his living warmth. 'You're sure you're not hurt? You haven't broken your ankle?'

'Nothing's wrong, I promise, except that I've got big feet.' He pulled a packet of candles from the pack and lit one. 'You'd better get going,' he said, 'and be careful, Jess. Don't *you* go falling. Remember you're my lifeline.' He gave a sad, crooked smile. 'In more ways than you realise!'

'I won't fall,' she promised. 'You stay out of mischief, I'll be as quick as I can.'

Outside, she undid her sunhat and hung it on the prickly-pear bush, so that she'd know which cave it was when she returned, and, holding the torch so that it gleamed steadily, she started to climb.

She was so relieved that he was safe, her feet seemed to have wings and she reached the summit in record time. Once in the car, a quick look at the map set her off in the direction of the nearest village. She drove fast, bouncing about dangerously on the uneven road, but soon she came to a hamlet and, drawing up at a rustic taverna, she attempted to get help.

She was in luck. The landlord at the inn spoke some English, and she managed to explain what had happened. A rope was fetched, and a crowbar, and a group of men, including the landlord, whose name was Yanni, piled into a lorry, eager to come to the aid of the English visitor.

Jess led them back to the cliffside, and together they scrambled down to the cave that she'd marked with her hat. After that, it was only a matter of minutes for the hefty Maniot men to lever the boulder and to haul Andros out.

At first he couldn't stand, for his foot was without sensation, but after much prodding and manipulating by Yanni the feeling came back and he felt he could manage the long climb.

'I should be in marvellous condition after today,' Jess panted as she hauled herself after him. 'I seem to have done nothing but climb up and down this ruddy cliff.'

'You're a remarkable girl,' he said, and he was very serious. 'Quite remarkable.'

He held out his hand and she took it without hesitation. She was exhausted, scratched, covered in dust and sweat, but the feeling between them was warm and sweet and she was content.

When they reached the summit, Andros insisted on driving back to Yanni's taverna and buying retsina for his liberators. 'And some dinner for us. I don't know about you,' he said to Jess, 'but I'm famished.'

She hadn't thought about it, but now she realised that she was not only weary, but also ravenous, and when they were in Yanni's shabby inn she fell on a plate of lamb stew with the appetite of a stevedore.

Their rescuers drank with them and there was much joking, laughing, and gurgling of bottles. Bread and olives and fruit were produced, and then some of the old men started telling stories. Ancient legends of the Mani, and the fables of the caves.

'Who was it found him first?' one of the old men asked, and when Jess was pointed out to him he came forward and placed her hand in Andros's.

The room fell silent. The old man said something softly and, lifting Andros's glass, spilled some of his wine over their joined hands. Then he spilt some of Jess's wine, so that the two wines mingled.

'What's he doing?' Jess whispered.

Andros whispered back, 'I think he's marrying us.'

'What?' She pulled her hand away, wiping at the wine with her hankie.

'Don't worry, it's not legal, but because you found me it seems we are now under the spell of the caves and bound to each other for life. The sprinkling with wine was for the benefit of the "evil ones". To keep the union safe.'

She gave a shaky laugh. 'Well, marriage and "evil ones" is a good combination,' she said lightly.

Andros looked at her thoughtfully. 'From various remarks you've made, I take it that you don't like marriage.'

'Frankly, I don't believe in it.'

He teased her, 'What a *modern* girl!' But his dark eyes were sober.

'Not modern at all. Just cautious,' she corrected. 'From what I've seen of the married state—and with a mother like mine I've seen plenty—one has about as much chance of making a marriage work as...as catching a rainbow!'

He reached for a dish of apricots and selected two, giving one to her. 'Poor Jess,' he said, so softly she could scarcely hear him. 'You really are one of the walking wounded.'

'After rushing up and down that cliff all day, what do you expect?' she replied, fighting to keep the conversation light-hearted, for banter she could deal with. It was sympathy she found hard to handle. Suppressing a gigantic yawn, she asked, 'Do you think we can leave without hurting anyone's feelings?'

'I'll see to it,' Andros said, and soon they were making their farewells and, after promises to come back to visit, they were on their way.

Back in the tower, Jess was so exhausted, it was all she could do to wash her face at the kitchen sink.

Andros took the towel form her and gently dabbed at her scratched face. 'Tomorrow, you sleep as long as you can,' he said firmly. He took her face flannel from her and guided her to the ladder. 'Up you go. You're clean enough for tonight.'

While she was struggling with the buttons on her shirt he came into her room, and when he helped her to slip it off her shoulders she was too tired to protest. 'Hold out your arms,' he said softly, smoothing ointment on to her cuts. Then he sat her down on the bed and pulled off her jeans. There was nothing sexual about the way he touched her; he seemed to only want to take care of her. 'Where's your nightie?'

She reached under the pillow and handed it to him, and he finished undressing her as tenderly as if she were a child. He turned back the sheet. 'In you get,' he murmured and Jess did as she was told, snuggling down blissfully.

'I seem to put you to bed a lot without ever climbing in myself,' he commented in an academic way, and when she started to say that she was sorry he whispered, 'Shhh! Go to sleep.' She felt the light touch of his fingers on her cheek before falling asleep.

She slept soundly till noon, when the sound of a car woke her. Andros had gone, leaving a note on the kitchen table and two pans of water heating on the stove. By the time he returned she was bathed, shampooed, and wearing a clean yellow cotton dress, her damp hair combed out over her shoulders. Coffee was ready on the stove, and a tray with mugs and a plate of biscuits waiting to be taken out into the shade.

He asked her if she was feeling rested, and she told him she was. 'And thanks for thinking of the hot water, that was thoughtful.' She was suddenly shy with him, remembering his gentle hands smoothing her, easing the clothes off her body.

It was another scorching day, but sitting in the shade of the walled yard was pleasant. They didn't talk much. There was no need for conversation. Jess had brought some paperwork out with her, and Andros was correcting his manuscript. A dog barked in the distance and a million cicadas buzzed away in the olive trees. Jess was at peace with the world.

What was it about this man? One moment he made her feel utterly relaxed, and the next moment she was in turmoil. She knew now that it was more than a sexual attraction. She'd been attracted to men before, but they had never affected her like this. Of all the men she'd known, Andros was the *one* man who was capable of making her vulnerable, and that frightened her, for hadn't her mother repeatedly told her that once a woman was vulnerable to a man she was lost?

Andros helped himself to more coffee and remarked chattily, 'The *Belle Hélène*'s docked at Yerolimin.'

'The what?'

'The yacht Gisele's cruising on.'

The fingers holding her pencil grew clammy. 'Did you see her?' she asked, underlining a word with unnecessary force.

'I saw the whole party.' He stretched out his long legs. 'We're going to join them for lunch and a sail tomorrow.'

He was doing it again! Taking over in that high-handed manner of his. Making plans without consulting her. And how about Gisele? How did she feel about it? Jess was pretty sure she wasn't over the moon at the thought of Andros bringing his secretary along. 'You'll have to go alone,' she said, frowning down at her notes. 'I'm much too busy.'

'Rubbish!' he said with characteristic arrogance. 'Only yesterday you were complaining because you didn't have enough to do.'

She put down her pencil. Her adrenalin was working overtime, and the peaceful atmosphere was shattered. 'I don't want to come,' she said.

'Not a good enough reason.' When he smiled in that superior way, she felt like emptying the coffee-pot over him.

'I think it is. I hate boats.' This was a blatant lie, but she didn't care.

'You'll like this one. And in the afternoon there'll be water-skiing.'

'Don't treat me like a child, Andros,' she said, tight-lipped.

'Don't behave like one, then,' he replied with infuriating reasonableness. She took a deep breath, ready to do battle, but he forestalled her by saying, 'Anyway, I want you to come. We can arrange about your plane ticket on the way.'

The bottom fell out of her world. 'Pl-plane ticket?'

He reached into the pocket of his shirt and brought out an airmail envelope. 'I collected the mail while I was in town,' he said, passing it to her. It was postmarked 'Australia'.

'From Kitty?' she asked.

'From *Mrs Armstrong*...Yes.'

So Kitty had married Charlie! Jess was glad for her. She wished her luck, but she also wished that, since Kitty had waited so long, she might have left it till the end of the summer before writing.

'She paid off the debt with two cheques, one post-dated,' Andros informed her. 'There was a heart-rending letter, too.' He raised an eye-brow comically. 'I gather Mr Armstrong read her the riot act when he found out what she'd done.'

'So you don't need collateral any more,' said Jess in a bright, thin voice.

'I don't need collateral,' he agreed. She looked down at the envelope in her hands and he went on, 'In any case, I now have enough material for the book. I must get back to running my business. I've neglected it long enough.'

She laid Kitty's letter on the tray. Who would have guessed that such a light piece of paper could deal such a body-blow! 'I should be able to finish the typing in a day or so,' she said.

'Of course, I shall give you wages until the end of the summer,' insisted Andros.

'That isn't necessary.' Oh, God! Did he suppose she was downcast because of a loss of *income*? 'You've been more than generous...'

'Nevertheless,' he said, 'I feel I owe you something.'

She repeated, 'That isn't necessary,' but he was adamant.

'And you must also have your medal,' he smiled.

'My *medal*?'

'For valour...and extreme forbearance.' He produced a small cardboard box from his other pocket. 'Not every girl would have rescued a boss who was as evil-tempered as I was yesterday.' He was really spelling out their relationship with all this talk of wages and bosses.

'What is it?'

'Only one way to find out.' He pushed the box towards her; inside was a gold medallion that hung on a slender chain. It had the figure of a woman engraved on one side.

'It's lovely, but I can't take it, Andros,' she said.

His mouth set in an obstinate line. 'Don't be discourteous, Jess,' he snapped. 'It's just a little memento from the Peloponnese, not the family emerald.'

Of course, he'd never give emeralds to his *secretary*, but it wasn't unusual for the boss to give a departing employee a small token, so why not just accept it and shut up? 'Well, thank you,' she said, looping the chain over her head. 'Who is the lady?'

'She's a nereid. She reminded me of you.'

She lifted the medallion and peered down at it. 'She looks a bit fierce.'

'So do you, at times.'

'It's lovely,' she said again. 'Thank you.'

'You are most welcome,' he replied gravely. 'And now, how about getting on with that typing? Get it out of the way so you can enjoy yourself tomorrow.'

It would take more than a clean desk to do that, but she said, 'Yes, *boss*!' smartly and went back towards the tower.

He called out, 'I won't be in for dinner tonight. I'm dining on the yacht.'

It was as if he had twisted a knife in her heart, but pride pulled her mouth into the travesty of a smile. 'Well, if I don't have a three-course meal to prepare, I should really be able to finish your notes!' she quipped.

'That's the spirit!' She thought he must still be feeling the strain of yesterday's adventure, for he looked rather bleak.

Some time later, when she was banging away on the typewriter in the office, he called goodbye and she heard the car drive off. She ripped out the page and put it on the growing pile beside her. She indulged briefly in the pain of imagining him with Gisele. Perhaps there would be dancing on board, and later he would go to her cabin. Take her in his arms...

And if he did she had no one to blame but herself, she told herself sternly. She had driven him away. She had driven him straight back to Gisele. She couldn't blame anyone but herself.

She sighed miserably. If only she could have explained her fears to him. Explained that her panic was stronger than ever before, because losing him would cause a wound that would never really heal. The hurt *now* was so intense that it made her ache, and their relationship was no deeper than a few kisses. Imagine how unbearable it would be if they had become lovers...

She inserted another sheet of paper into the typewriter and went back to copying his notes, and the typewriter keys tapped out a rhythm that beat time drearily with her heart. A dirge of her own making.

CHAPTER EIGHT

As ANDROS had said they would, they arranged for her flight back to England on their way to lunch. It seemed awfully easy to do, Jess thought dismally. One phone call to his office, a quick coffee at a taverna, and the office had called back to say she was scheduled on a flight to Gatwick the following afternoon. She looked out across the sunlit bay, and already she had the feeling that there was a touch of autumn in the air. For her, summer was ending.

'Your ticket will be waiting at the airport,' Andros said, his voice without expression.

'Well, I'll be back in good time for registration for my course,' she said brightly, her heart sinking like a lift.

'Your course?'

'Mmm! So I can move on to better things.' She managed a narrow smile. 'Typing your material has been fun, but I'd like something more challenging than typing for the future.'

'You've got a good brain, Jess,' he said. 'I'll be happy to give you a reference.'

Oh! he was so businesslike and formal, she felt the life was being squeezed out of her. 'Thank you.'

He stood up. Today he was wearing his white trousers and a faded green shirt that had once been expensive but had seen better days. He hadn't had a haircut for weeks and his hair curled on his brown neck. He looked like a tousled little boy, and Jess found it hard not to touch him; ruffle his hair, stroke his cheek.

'We'd better get going,' he said, rising to his feet. 'Mustn't keep the party waiting,' and Jess thought he meant that he mustn't keep Gisele waiting.

The *Belle Hélène* was a big surprise. She had realised that any yacht that cruised around the Greek Islands would be larger than Tony's sloop, but she wasn't prepared for this one. First of all, she didn't carry any sail, and to Jess 'yacht' was synonymous with 'sail', but the *Belle Hélène* was a power yacht. White and sleek, she practically took over the entire harbour of Yerolimin, her teak decks spotless, her paintwork brilliant in the sun, looking for all the world like an infant *Queen Elizabeth*. A member of her crew, dressed in a smart white uniform, helped them aboard, and then a rotund lady, clad in a tentlike dress, her hair a startling shade of blue, bore down on them. 'Andy, honey! You made it!' she exclaimed in a ringing American accent.

'You don't think I'd miss one of your famous lunches, do you, Myra?' smiled Andros.

'And this is Jess?' enquired the blue-haired lady.

He nodded. 'This is Jess. And, drawing Jess forward, he introduced her. 'This is our hostess, Jess, the Baroness Brücken.'

The Baroness took Jess's hand in her own beringed one. 'Welcome aboard, honey! You're very welcome!' she said. Looking keenly at Jess, at her mass of silky toffee-coloured hair and shapely young body, she added, 'I gotta hand it to you, Andy, you sure know how to pick 'em!'

'*There* you are *liebling*!' They turned to see Gisele standing at a cabin door, staring at them, her green eyes glittering dangerously. 'I have been waiting for you.'

'You shoulda come up on deck, Gisele…piped him aboard, if you were so anxious,' Myra Brücken remarked easily. 'Have you met Miss Firbank yet?'

'I have met Andros's secretary, yes,' replied the German woman, and then she asked, 'Do you intend to work this afternoon, Andros? Is that why you bring your secretary along?'

'I thought I'd give her the day off,' said Andros, his face blank. 'I thought it might be fun for her.'

'I'm sure the crew will be delighted to make her welcome,' Gisele murmured. 'And now, Lord and Lady Alchester are most anxious to make your acquaintance.'

'Let's all go to the aft deck for drinks,' their hostess said sharply, 'then if any of the crew wants to meet Jess they can do it while they serve her lunch.' She tucked her arm firmly into Jess's. 'C'mon, honey! Come and meet the gang.'

Gisele made a kind of hissing sound high in her nose, and grabbed Andros's arm as he followed the Baroness.

There were a lot of people gathered on the aft deck, some lounging in basket chairs, tall glasses in their hands, others leaning against the rail. Lord and Lady Alchester, an English couple who managed to look as if they were wearing tweeds in spite of their summer cottons, were introduced, and their daughter Felicity, a fresh-faced girl of twenty, gave Jess a friendly smile and made room for her on the wicker sofa. Gisele deposited herself on a chair opposite and tried to pull Andros down next to her, but he took a seat beside Myra Brücken.

Drinks were ordered and Jess quietly studied the party gathered around her. They were a polyglot group. Greeks, Germans, Americans. Everyone casually dressed in beach clothes that quietly screamed of money. This didn't bother Jess; she was not the type to be cowed by the trappings of wealth. She knew she looked trim and attractive in her blue cotton dress with the daisies on it, her skin tanned to a rich golden brown, and her hair streaked and gilded by the sun, and since Jess's greatest talent was the ability to mix well with all kinds of people she was soon chatting away to Felicity as if they were old friends.

Felicity wanted to know how long she had worked for Andros, and what she'd done before coming to Greece. When Jess told her she had been a barmaid in a pub in Brighton, Gisele looked up from her drink and said loudly, 'Is that where you met Andros? In a public house?'

'Jess and I met in Greece,' Andros replied for Jess. 'In Vathia, actually.' His mouth grew tender. 'I looked over the parapet and there she was.'

'Well, fate was sure kind to you, Andy,' Myra said, 'to plant such a looker on your doorstep.'

And Lord Alchester said, 'Yes, indeed,' and smoothed his whiskers appreciatively.

Gisele banged her glass down on the glass-topped table so hard it was a miracle it didn't shatter. Several of the guests stopped talking and stared.

'I was in Athens last week, Andros,' the German woman said. 'I had lunch with your cousin while I was there.'

'With George?' said Andros, leaning back in his chair. 'I trust he's keeping his nose to the grindstone.'

'George is charming and very gallant,' said Gisele severely, and she added in an undertone, 'He was also very informative.' Her cold green eyes rested on Jess, who felt like a rabbit being eyed by a stoat.

Lunch was a buffet—set up on a sideboard that ran the length of the dining-room, with food that would have done justice to any four-star hotel. Small tables had been set for the guests in the main lounge, in which there was a bar, a games table, a music centre, and a colour television with video recorder. There was a big sofa and matching chairs covered in oyster-coloured suede, and a white carpet, as soft and springy as a meadow, covered the floor. Brass lamps and bright lacquer gleamed discreetly.

'Wow!' Jess whispered to Andros as she helped herself to lobster salad. 'I can see why you never miss one of the Baroness's luncheons. This is a far cry from bread and cheese in the yard.'

He paused in the act of spooning some caviar on to his plate. 'I enjoy our simple lunches,' he said.

'So do I.' She generously helped herself to scampi. 'But I must say, this kind of luxury makes a pleasant change. Is this boat new? I've never seen anything like it.'

'Fairly new. Myra's had the boat since last year. It's her latest toy.'

'What about the Baron?'

'He's dead,' said Andros bluntly. 'He left Myra very well off, and she's been clever with investments.'

'I can believe *that*.' She peered closely at a Lalique vase. 'You'd need to be pretty clever to afford this lot.'

He began to steer her towards one of the tables. 'I suppose I'm used to this sort of thing,' he said. 'That's why life at the tower is such a pleasure.'

That's one in the eye for you, Jess, she thought. He's telling you—as tactfully as he can—that you come from a different world.

Out of the corner of her eye, she saw Felicity gesturing to the one chair left at her table. 'I said I'd eat lunch with Felicity and her friends,' she said, and he gave her a frigid bow before going to join Gisele.

She'd done it again! Thrown him straight back into Gisele's arms. The minute he tries to get close, you push him away, she thought bitterly. Jess's shuttle service! It's the pattern of my life. This took away all appetite, and the delicious food suddenly had all the allure of boiled cardboard.

She had to make a determined effort to join in the fun around her table, for the two young American boys Felicity had dragooned as lunch companions seemed awfully callow, and she had to work hard to appear amused. She also had to work hard not to look too often over at Andros, who seemed to be in great form if the laughter from his table was anything to go by. Gisele's red head was practically on his shoulder, and from time to time her hand would close over his. Jess would dearly liked to have buried her fish knife in it!

Coffee was served on deck, and she took her cup to the rail to escape both the Americans *and* the sight of Gisele cosying up to Andros.

Felicity came over to her. 'We'll be casting off any moment,' she said, 'so we'll be clear of the harbour for water skiing.'

'It should be cooler, too,' Jess remarked, for the sun was beating down so that even the blue and white striped awning that was stretched over the deck gave little relief.

'You can rest in my cabin if you're too hot,' Felicity suggested. 'It's air-conditioned.'

'Thanks, but I'm fine.' She finished her coffee. 'It's just that noon does tend to get a bit sticky in these parts.'

'I wondered if you were feeling all right. You looked a bit downcast at lunch,' Felicity said, and Jess silently cursed those quick young eyes.

'I'm just a bit tired,' she said. 'I've been working at quite a pace.'

A steward took the girls' cups, and then they leaned side by side on the rail as the crew cast off and the *Belle Hélène* started cruising away from Vathia.

'That's nice,' said Jess, when a light breeze lifted the hair off her forehead.

'I didn't think you were the kind who got bothered by the heat,' her companion remarked. 'I mean, you're so brown. Not like me.' She eyed her pale arm with disgust. 'The sun turns me into a lobster.'

Jess grinned. 'Come on! I bet you make a very pretty lobster.'

'Oh, do you really think so?' Felicity brightened. 'You are a lamb. I only wish Brad thought so, too.' Brad was one of the young Americans.

'It matters what Brad thinks, does it?' Jess asked, and the girl nodded emphatically.

'*Desperately!* I'm madly in love with him. But *madly!* It's hell.'

'It must be!'

'Are you in love?'

Much too loudly, Jess said, '*No!*'

'You don't have to be so vehement, Jess,' said Felicity, looking startled. 'I just thought you might be in love with Andros.' Jess felt her cheeks starting to burn. 'I mean, he is so *divinely* dishy, isn't he?'

'Yes . . . yes, I suppose he is,' Jess agreed weakly.

'Not as good-looking as Brad, of course, but so *masculine*. Quite divine.'

Shut up, shut up, shut *up*! screamed Jess silently, but she simply nodded and smiled vaguely at the girl.

'Look at that cow, Gisele! She's practically sitting in his lap,' Felicity drawled. 'She really is the *end*. I think she's a perfect cow, don't you?'

Jess replied diplomatically, 'I don't really know her,' but couldn't resist adding, 'I must admit, she's not my favourite lady.'

'*Lady!* Ha!' Felicity exploded. 'I could tell you stories about *that* one that would make your hair curl.'

'Well, don't. I prefer my hair the way it is.' She didn't want to hear any gossip about Gisele. Just the sight of her, leaning across Andros in that intimate way, the sound of her tinkling laugh, was hard enough to stomach; she didn't need to hear lurid tales about her as well.

The party broke up for a siesta soon after this. Most of the guests went below to their cabins to rest. Those remaining stretched themselves out on the comfortable lounge chairs that were dotted around the upper decks.

'I will not sleep,' Gisele told Andros. 'Why do you not come to my stateroom? I could show you those photographs of Davos.' She drooped her eyes seductively.

Andros, however, refused. 'I was up at the crack of dawn, darling,' he said. 'I need a nap. Particularly if I'm to perform on water-skis.'

'Isn't it rather difficult on water-skis?' Jess asked *sotto voce*, and he chuckled.

'Before you take your nap, Andy,' Myra said, 'I want you to come and see the new radar equipment I've had installed. The captain's wild about it, he's just tickled pink.' She led Andros away and Jess was left with Gisele.

The German woman gave her a blank, arrogant stare. 'There may be a bunk free in the crews' quarters,' she said.

'No, thank you, I'll stay on deck,' said Jess. Gisele's antagonism was as palpable as scent. Why doesn't she lay off? Jess wondered. She's Andros's woman, what more does she want?

Gisele started for the companionway, then turned back. 'Let me give you a warning, Miss...er...'

'Firbank.'

'Firbank. Yes.' Her eyes were green slits as she hissed, 'If necessary, I shall not hesitate to tell the Baroness what I have learned of your past, to prevent you from insinuating your way into our society.'

Jess shrugged her slim shoulders. 'You do whatever you want,' she said.

Gisele looked livid. 'Do not take that tone with me,' she grated. 'Remember that your little summer is nearly over, and then Andros will not even remember your name.'

That hurt, in fact, it nearly made Jess flinch, but she said, as calmly as she could, 'I don't really think that's any business of yours.'

'Anything to do with Andros concerns me,' said Gisele, 'particularly when I see him being taken in by an unscrupulous woman.'

'You mean me?'

'It would not be the first time that a simple, innocent man became the victim of a scheming slut.'

Jess opened her gray eyes wide at this unlikely description of Andros.

'I am *varning* you,' fumed Gisele, her English slipping with her temper, 'you will not find it so amusing if I decide to reveal your past.'

'Oh, buzz off!' said Jess, for she had suddenly had enough of this tedious woman.

She left Gisele standing speechless with rage in the companionway, and found an empty deck-chair well away from the other guests. She was still ruffled by that nasty, bullying scene. Obviously Gisele must have learnt about the pawned emerald, but didn't know that the money had been repaid.

She looked moodily over the calm water which glistened like silk in the brilliant sun. It was bad enough leaving Andros, without having his mistress nattering away at her, she thought bitterly. Bad enough, that in forty-eight hours she would be back at the gentler Sussex coast, with no imperious, humorous Andros, a lovely thorn in her side.

Myra Brücken's nasal voice brought her back from this dismal reverie. 'Not sleepin', honey? Then I guess you won't mind if I join you.' She eased herself into an adjacent chair. 'Phew! It sure is hot. Too hot to nap, eh?'

'It certainly is warm,' agreed Jess, putting her unopened book away.

Her hostess kicked off her sandals. 'Andy sure was impressed with the radar,' she said, wriggling her plump little toes. 'He thinks this boat is real neat.'

'It is lovely,' said Jess, wondering where Andros was now. Bouncing about with Gisele on a bunk somewhere, probably.

'Have you enjoyed working for Andros?' Myra asked.

'Very much,' said Jess, being careful to neutralise her voice, 'and of course it's been super, being in Greece.'

'I bet,' said the Baroness, 'and I know you've been a great help to him. He was telling me.'

'That's nice.' She'd get a good reference. Sternly, she told herself to be grateful for that.

'I used to be a stenographer,' remarked Myra. 'That's how I met Otto...the Baron. I was his secretary when he opened his business in the States.'

'Really?' She rather wished Myra hadn't joined her; she wasn't in the mood for a chat.

'Yeah! He was a great little guy.' Myra's harsh voice grew softer. 'I really miss him. We met and married in six weeks.' She gave a reminiscent chuckle. 'The ruckus when that happened! A guy like Otto marrying a *steno*! His friends were in conniptions!'

Jess smiled. 'And now?'

'What do *you* think, honey? Now they're sweet as candy. They can't *wait* for an invitation from the *Baroness*. It slays me! Otto always got a bang out of it when he was alive.' She twisted her wedding ring around thoughtfully. 'He couldn't abide a snob. He was an OK guy. You woulda liked him.'

'I'm sure I would,' Jess said.

'Andy reminds me of him in a lot of ways,' said the Baroness. 'Oh, not to look at, of course. Otto didn't have Andy's looks. But he was completely honest and up-front...just like Andy. They were real fond of each other.'

'They knew each other, then?'

'Oh, sure! Otto had business dealings with the Kalimantis firm, and he took a regular shine to Andy.' She examined the rings sparkling on her fingers. 'When Otto passed away, Andy was real good to me,' she said, 'helping me with the business side of things, and letting me bawl on his shoulder when I needed to. He's a very sensitive guy...but moody. Well, heck! He's half-Greek, what do you expect?' She stopped examining her jewellery. 'Can I ask you somethin' personal, honey? Do you like Andy...I mean, *really* like him? You know.'

'You mean, am I in love with him?' Jess was unnerved to find that her heart was pumping painfully. Was it going to be like this every time Andros's name was mentioned?

Myra nodded her blue head. Jess had never had a mother she could confide in; she was used to keeping her own counsel, solving her own problems, so she was surprised to discover that before she could stop herself she had admitted that she did indeed love Andros.

'But it's no good,' she said miserably, 'it would never work. Besides...there's Gisele.'

'That tacky broad?' Myra exploded. 'You don't hafta worry about *her*! She's nothing but a jet-set hanger-on. She invited herself on this cruise, and if I'd had a brain in my head I would have told her to get lost!'

It was not unpleasant to hear Gisele attacked, but Jess felt compelled to try and explain. 'It isn't only that, Baroness. It's me...Oh, God! I don't know...' She shook her barley-coloured head. 'I...I don't really want to talk about it.'

Myra Brücken took Jess's hand in her soft plump one. 'I won't push you, honey, but I will give you a bit of advice. Don't throw away a chance of happiness. Gisele means nothing to Andy. I *know*. I also know he cares for you, so if you want him, don't be dumb. OK?'

Before Jess had a chance to answer, Felicity's head poked up from the lower deck stairs. 'Time for water skiing,' she sang out cheerily.

Jess had to admit that her timing was awful for, even though it got her off Myra's conversational hook, the prospect of watching Andros and Gisele sport about like dolphins didn't exactly thrill her, so she said, 'I don't know how to water-ski, I think maybe I'll give it a miss.'

Felicity refused to be put off. 'Don't be dreary, Jess. Hurry up! You have to put on a bathing suit. You can change in my cabin.' She had already changed into a one-piece suit and was wearing a short towelling robe. So, collecting her big straw bag, Jess meekly followed her.

The cabin was roomy, luxurious, and excessively untidy. 'Forgive the mess,' said Felicity, picking a bundle of silky underwear up from the white shag carpet and slinging it on the bed. 'We only brought one maid with us, and she spends all her time doing things for Mummy.'

'Poor you! Don't tell me you have to make your own bed, too!' teased Jess, starting to undress.

Felicity grinned. 'What a nice colour your bikini is,' she remarked. 'It looks simply marvellous with your tan.'

'You look very nice yourself. White skin is very attractive, you know.'

Felicity peered at herself morosely in the glass. 'I hope so. Do you know, Jess, I couldn't have *borne* facing Brad without you around to give me courage. He makes me feel so... so *limp*.'

'I thought being in love was supposed to make you feel marvellous,' Jess said, tying up her bikini bra and adjusting the shoulder-straps.

'It's just that he's so *gorgeous*.' Felicity picked up a pair of eyebrow tweezers from the chaos on the dressing-table and plucked out a straggling hair. 'I saw him on deck when I came to fetch you. He's wearing the *teeniest* pair of trunks. I turned to jelly, it's *too* shame making!'

Jess draped a shocking pink towel over her shoulders. 'Do you fall in love often?' she asked, as the two of them headed for the door.

'*Constantly!* The killing thing is that in a week I'll probably be over it,' Felicity replied sunnily. 'Mummy says it's a phase.'

'Reminds me of... of someone I know,' Jess said, repressing a shudder.

By now, the *Belle Hélène* had cruised several miles. The captain had shut off the motor, so that they lay becalmed on a surface as unruffled as a bowl of milk. The two small power-boats that were carried midships had been lowered into the water, ready for the water skiing.

The guests were gathered on the aft deck. Gisele was wearing a bikini made of some kind of silky material printed to look like snakeskin, which Jess thought very reptilian and appropriate.

Andros was in the power-boat, his powerful body glittering with drops of water, for he had already been swimming. His hair, which had been sleeked flat, was just starting to spring up in unruly curls again.

They all climbed down into the little boats, with the exception of Myra Brücken. 'I'm not the build for boats like that,' she told them.

Jess tried to hold back, so that she wouldn't be in the same boat as Gisele and Andros, but Andros spied her lurking behind a group of Americans and called out that there was plenty of room in his boat, so, outwardly compliant but inwardly fuming, she took his outstretched hand and climbed in.

He was the first to ski and he was very good. He swung back and forth across the wake, seeming at times to ski alongside the power-boat as it zoomed over the water. Whenever he did this, Gisele would wave delightedly. Jess remained stolidly unimpressed by this display of unmitigated showing-off. Even when he only used one ski, she refused to applaud. Let Gisele feed his ego, if that was what he wanted!

After several minutes he let go of the line and trod water, waiting for the boat to pick him up, but Gisele insisted that another line be attached so that they could ski together.

And this they did for nearly fifteen minutes, for Gisele was as good as he was. Watching them skimming behind the boat, Andros so tanned and strong and Gisele creamy pale against the foam, Jess grew more depressed than ever. It was all very well for Myra Brücken to say Gisele meant nothing to him, but it was more likely that, given her background, Myra sentimentalised about secretaries and their employers, and that blinded her to the truth.

At last they climbed back into the boat. Gisele picked up one of the fluffy white towels, piped in the same blue as the trim on the *Belle Hélène.*

'Andros and I ski well together,' she informed them unnecessarily. With a look at Jess, she patted her towel sensuously down his muscled chest, mopping up the drops that clung to his dark hair. Then she dropped the towel and let her hand rest on his tanned midriff, just above the top of his trunks. 'We do many things well together,' she said softly.

Jess—who had never felt a jealous pang in her life— stared down at that insolent hand and was suddenly pierced with hatred. She would like to have sunk her teeth into it and drawn blood; gone for the German woman with nails and fists, and generally behaved in an uncivilised manner.

Shaken by the ferocity of this emotion, she leaned over the side of the boat and gazed determinedly down at the translucent water that was the colour of an aquamarine. Soon she would be looking at a different sea, at greyer, colder water. Her life, too, would be colder, without Andros near her. And the awful thing was that it was all her own doing. She was the one who had engineered this vacuum, and it was too late now to do anything about it.

The skiing seemed to go on interminably, and when it was her turn she did not do well, for Andros had volunteered to coach her and all she could concentrate on was the touch of his hands as he helped her put on the skis, and the sight of his lithe body when he hauled himself out of the water.

At last they headed back to the *Belle Hélène*, where Myra was waiting to serve them tea on the journey back to Yerolimin.

Jess changed into her blue dress and twisted her damp hair into a knot on top of her head before going on deck to join the party. She wished she could have stayed in Felicity's cabin, away from Gisele's hostile scrutiny. Away from Andros...

'There you are, honey!' Myra called from behind a gigantic silver tea service. 'What do you like in your tea? Milk or lemon?'

Jess accepted her cup and went to sit a little way off, but Myra insisted she take a chair beside her, which meant Jess was sitting across the table from Gisele and Andros.

'I've been trying to get Andy to stick around when we get to port,' Myra said. 'I'd like you both to stay for dinner. But Andy tells me you have to get back to pack, because you're leaving for England tomorrow. Is that right?'

'And you, *liebling*,' said Gisele, a wave of perfume wafting from her cleavage, 'you will be staying on in Greece?'

Andros, his eyes fixed steadily on Jess, said lazily, 'Only for a couple of days—in Athens—then I must get back to the London office.'

'But that is splendid! I myself plan to be in London. We shall be able to see much of each other.'

Jess would have bet her summer's salary that Gisele had only just made those plans.

'Don't bank on it, Gisele,' Andros replied pleasantly. 'I'm going to be pretty well tied up.'

Gisele's thin lips grew thinner. 'I shall endeavour to untie you, then,' she said.

'The knots that are tying me don't come loose that easily,' he said, his black eyes still fixed unwaveringly on Jess.

'Before you go, Jess,' said the Baroness, 'we must exchange addresses. I sure don't want to lose touch with you.'

'I don't, either,' Felicity chimed in, 'you must come and visit us in the country. Mustn't she, Mummy?'

'You would be advised to lock up your jewellery during Miss Firbank's visit,' said Gisele loudly, and the chatter around the table ceased.

Jess felt as if the blood was draining out of her body.

'What the hell are you talking about?' asked Andros, and Jess shivered at his tone.

Gisele went on, 'When I met George in Athens, he told me that Miss Firbank and another girl tricked him into parting with a valuable ring which they later stole. I simply tell you this as a warning,' she said to the Baroness, 'for it is clear that this . . . *girl* is very clever at insinuating herself in decent society . . .'

Myra said, 'Just a goddammed minute!' but Gisele was not to be stopped.

'. . . and fooling people with her . . . *charm. Mein Gott,* look at you!' she suddenly shrieked at Andros. 'You are *besotted* with the creature. She has bewitched you, and now you cannot see her for the cheap whore she is!'

Andros's chair fell to the ground with a clatter and he sprang to his feet, grabbing Gisele's shoulders in a vicelike grip. Everybody at the table became very still.

'You lying bitch,' he snarled. 'You wouldn't recognise honest charm if you fell over it! All your life you've schemed and connived, and now you're livid because your plan to seduce me into paying your debts for you hasn't worked.' He released her arm and stood away, white-faced and trembling. 'I'd throw you overboard if I didn't think it would poison the fish! Get out of my sight before I change my mind.'

Gisele gave a strangled choke of rage. 'I will not forget this,' she hissed at Jess before hurling herself down the companionway to the cabins below.

'I think maybe we should order fresh tea!' said Myra, beckoning the steward who had been watching, fascinated.

'I...I don't think I want any more, thank you,' said Jess, who suddenly felt shaky.

'Hey, look! Nobody believed all that stuff Gisele was spouting,' Myra assured her.

And Felicity said quickly, 'Of *course* we didn't. Gisele is a spiteful *cow*...we all know that.'

Andros came over to Jess and put his arm around her. 'Why don't we go and stand in the bow for a bit?' he said. 'Just you and me. Clean this ugliness out of our heads.'

'You do that,' said Myra, 'and then don't give it another thought, Jess. You hear?'

Impulsively, Jess put her arms around Myra's cushiony body and gave her a hug.

'Off you go!' She gave her a motherly pat. 'Andy! You take care of her now!'

'I will,' he promised, gently leading her away.

When they stood in the bow he said, 'I'm sorry, Jess. I blame myself for that sordid scene just now. *I* must have put the idea that we'd been tricked into George's head.' His face was tight with distress. 'I never dreamed he'd talk to Gisele about it.'

She leaned wearily against the rail. 'I wish Kitty had never come to me for help,' she said, 'then I'd never have known about that wretched emerald.'

'Or met me.' He looked stricken.

She couldn't bear him to look like that, and without thinking she gave a low cry, 'Oh, no! No, Andros!' And before she knew it she was in his arms and he was raining kisses on her cheeks, murmuring her name.

Her hair started to tumble down and he took the hairpins out of it and flung them over the side. 'Don't, my sweet,' he whispered when her great eyes filled with tears. 'Don't! I can't bear it when you cry.'

However, she didn't stop immediately, but allowed herself the comfort of leaning against him, letting her tears soak into her green shirt before she straightened up and said gruffly, 'Sorry about that.'

'Darling, don't go all formal on me again,' he beseeched her. 'This is the first time you've clung to me since that afternoon on the beach. Don't turn away from me again.'

'But you and Gisele,' she protested. 'I thought you and Gisele were...'

'I had this idiotic idea that perhaps I could make you jealous.' He let her go and scraped his hands through his hair. 'Not a very worthy plan, I admit, but I was desperate, Jess. I would have tried *anything* to get a reaction from you.'

Jess began to feel a glimmer of sympathy for her rival. 'Poor Gisele,' she said.

'Save your pity. The only thing she cares about is the Kalimantis money. It was the same before.'

'Before?'

'Many moons ago, Gisele and I had a brief—and not very happy—affair. It finished when I discovered what a gold-digger she was. She subsequently discovered a wealthier lover, but now he's ditched her and she's on the prowl again.' Jess looked up into his sloe-black eyes. 'There have been women in my past, Jess. I'm thirty-one, after all!'

She said quickly, 'You don't have to explain, Andros.'

As quickly, he replied, 'But I *do*. I'm the one who brought you on this blasted day-trip. It's my fault you were exposed to Gisele's bitchiness. Myra said it wouldn't work.'

'Myra?'

'Last night, I talked for hours to Myra about you. Told her how I felt.'

And she'd imagined him dancing with Gisele—taking her to bed! 'And now it's too late,' she said dolefully, 'I'm going home tomorrow.'

'My darling idiot!' he said. 'There's no law that says we can only be together in Greece.'

He tilted her chin so that she was forced to look at him. 'You do...care for me...don't you, Jess? Just a little?'

Her heart turned over with desire and her years of carefully learnt caution deserted her as, flinging herself in his arms, she cried out, 'Oh, yes! Yes, Andros. I do!'

CHAPTER NINE

THEY stayed on the bow of the *Belle Hélène* for the journey back to Yerolimin. No one bothered them. Myra, guessing that they wanted to be alone, saw to that.

Leaning side by side, Andros's arm round her waist, they watched the *Belle Hélène*'s prow cut through sea that was the colour of polished jade. After a while, a school of dolphins came and gambolled around the vessel, leaping out of the water and plunging and spiralling, to vanish at last like swift shadows. Then they would materialise again and sail in the air in another great arc, streamlined and sleek, from their elegant, smiling snouts to the clean-cut flukes of their tails. After a few more incredible loops and dives, they suddenly turned and vanished, dying away along the sea's floor like ghosts.

'Oh!' breathed Jess. 'They were so beautiful.'

'They say here that the day you see the dolphins play will be a day like no other.' He looked down at her tenderly. 'We know that's true now, don't we, my darling?'

She nodded and nestled closer, but for the first time since her passionate declaration of love her old demons of uncertainty were beginning to surface again. She was so happy, how on earth would she cope if it went wrong? What if Andros stopped caring for her? She felt as if a tiny cloud had appeared on her personal horizon. No more than a wisp of vapour right now, but a cloud, nevertheless.

There was an awkward moment when they got into port, when Gisele, followed by two stewards bearing a mountain of luggage, stamped down the gangplank.

Andros returned her hostile stare and tightened his grip on Jess.

'And good riddance!' said Myra, who had joined them when the boat docked. 'I told her right out she was no longer welcome aboard my boat.' She pressed Jess to her copious bosom. 'I'm not gonna say goodbye, honey—just, so long! Andy will be bringing you for a visit before we know it!'

Jess smiled and murmured, 'I hope so,' although she wasn't so sure.

Felicity insisted on walking with them to the car. 'Don't forget about coming to visit me,' she reminded Jess, tearing a page from her address book and writing down her phone number. 'We'll be home in a fortnight.'

'I'll have to get myself organised with my classes.' Jess carefully tucked the piece of paper in her purse. She probably wouldn't phone. Her life-style didn't really fit in with the likes of Lord and Lady Alchester's.

Sensing her reluctance, Felicity insisted. '*You* bring her, Andros. You know Mummy and Daddy are always pleased to see you.'

'Well, I'm certainly not coming without Jess.' He installed her in the passenger seat and got behind the wheel. 'Goodbye, Felicity,' he said firmly. 'Have a nice time on the rest of your holiday.'

Felicity beamed. 'Oh, I *will*! Brad told me I had a cute bottom this morning!'

'Well, *that's* progress!' chuckled Jess, waving as Andros put the car into gear and they roared off towards the mountains.

'She's a nice child,' said Andros, 'but I thought we'd *never* get away.' He stole a glance at Jess. Her hair was streaming out behind her in the breeze from the open sunroof, a curtain of dark blonde silk. 'How lovely you are,' he said softly.

Jess looked down at her clasped hands. She was breathing shallowly. It was, she thought, a miracle she

could breathe at all, her heart was racing so hard. Soon
they would be back in Vathia, back in the privacy of the
tower, and then Andros would take her in his arms and
make love to her. She was trembling like an aspen leaf
with desire... and panic. Supposing he lost interest once
they had made love... or they discovered that they were
hopelessly unsuited? Her hands were clammy in spite of
the warmth of the late afternoon.

As they drove back on the familiar road to Vathia,
she looked at the passing scenery intently, trying to im-
print it on to her memory, so she would be able to recall
it in the months ahead. During the long English winter
she wanted to be able to shut her eyes and picture the
strange village of towers climbing up the barren
mountainside. Picture Andros, strong and brown in his
tattered shorts, his hair falling tousled over his broad
brow, his moustache a black bar above his sensual lips,
because it was possible that after tonight a memory
would be all that remained for her.

Back in the tower, Andros opened all the trap doors,
so that the late afternoon sunlight flooded into the
kitchen, gleaming on to the whitewashed walls. Jess stood
irresolute in the middle of all this light.

Coming over to her, he tilted her chin so that he could
search her face. 'It's nearly time for the sunset.' He
stroked her hair. 'How about a drink on the tower, to
toast the night?'

She nodded, grateful that he wasn't rushing her, and
fetched a bottle of ouzo while he filled a jug with cold
water. Putting two stubby glasses in his trouser pockets,
he stood by the ladder. 'Up you go,' he said, 'or we'll
miss the sunset.' And, carefully holding the jug, he followed her.

It was the time of day when the white glare of sunlight
had turned to a curtain of golden satin, softening the
landscape, rounding the edges of the jagged mountains.
Jess walked over to the parapet and looked out towards

the coast. A row of twinkling lights sailing westwards slid out of the lee. A cruise ship, maybe? Alive with laughter and music. Perhaps people were leaning on the rail, looking ashore at the wild and secret mountains, thinking how lonely it must be, never dreaming that in that wilderness a girl was waiting for the touch of her lover's lips—torn between apprehension and desire.

'Our last Greek sunset,' he said, putting his arm round her shoulders. She could smell the scent of his flesh, see the texture of his skin, and she wondered if she would faint with longing. 'Don't look so sad, darling. We'll be back.' And turning her to face him, he kissed her gently on the mouth.

It was as if he drew all feeling out of her body into her lips as he kissed her; her anxiety disappeared and she clung to him, winding her arms round his neck so that they were as close as two flames.

Her lips parted, and her body went slack against his. They slipped down on to the ground, but she was unaware of the sun-warmed stone, the glow from the setting sun. Unaware of anything but his mouth, and the desire which claimed her in a surge of flame.

He unbuttoned her dress and slipped it from her shoulders, his lips trailing kisses over her neck, her breasts...

'You're so beautiful, my darling,' he murmured hoarsely, and she slid her hands into his open shirt, exulting in the rough feel of hair and smooth, warm skin under her fingers, revelling in her delight as her hands explored his body.

He groaned aloud, and now when he brought his mouth down on hers his kisses were fervent and she was transfigured with passion.

With his skilful touch he urged her on to greater pleasure, until she felt she was being swept along in a fast-moving current, faster and faster, until she was poised for a moment, like a frozen waterfall, until they fell together, back to the warm earth below.

They lay still for a long time, wrapped in each other's arms, then he slid to her side, and stroked her cheek. 'You are the most beautiful woman in the world,' he whispered, 'and to think we wasted a whole summer.' He kissed the tip of her nose. 'We'll have to make up for lost time.'

Jess leaned happily against his naked shoulder. 'Mmm!'

'But in a softer place. I didn't exactly plan this. I really did mean it when I invited you up here to admire the sunset.'

She giggled. 'What sunset?' For now the stars had come out and the sky was velvety black above them. She traced her fingers slowly down his chest, sensuously revelling in the feel of his crisp, dark hair. All her doubts had vanished. She had never felt this way in her life before. Never felt so complete.

Eventually they dressed, stopping to kiss every few seconds, still filled with the wonder of their lovemaking.

'There's something I have to explain to you, Jess,' Andros said, when they were sitting on the parapet drinking ouzo, their arms still linked because they couldn't bear to stop touching each other.

'You don't have to explain anything, darling.' She snuggled closer. 'We don't need words.'

He kissed the top of her silky head. 'Sweetheart, I do.' He gently moved her away. 'You once accused me of having an obsession about blackmail. Do you remember?'

Nodding, she said, 'I remember, but it doesn't matter any...'

He laid his finger on her lips. 'Shh! I must tell you, Jess. I accused you unjustly once and I feel badly.'

'You don't need to,' she said. 'Not any more.'

'I know that, but I want you to know *why* I was so hasty in my judgement. Why I was so unfair to you.'

She searched his face for some indication of what was in his mind. 'Have you been blackmailed in the past, then?'

He didn't answer her question right away, but said after a few seconds, 'My parents had a good marriage. They liked the same people and shared the same tastes, in all respects but one—Greece. My mother dislikes this country. She could never adjust to the life here, and when I was at boarding-school in England she spent more and more time away from Athens...and her husband.'

He took his arm out of Jess's and stared into the night. 'I was just fifteen. My father was having business difficulties at that time, and he was at a...a difficult age.' He raked his hand through his hair in that gesture she recognised now as one of distress.

'I'm not trying to make excuses for him,' he went on. 'He was foolish. But he was also...human...and lonely. He met a woman one night at a club on the Plaka. She was young and pretty, and my father was flattered that such a young girl should pay him attention. He took her back to our—empty—apartment, and she stayed for the weekend.

'I know that my father was not lying to me when he said that he felt relief when she left. It had been an interlude in his life that he was not proud of.'

He fell silent and Jess whispered, 'What happened?'

'A few days later, she came back. She wanted money. My father was prominent in both the business and the political community in Athens, and she threatened to go to the papers. To say that he had kept her against her will. Had forced her to submit to all kinds of...of *filth*, and that she had been too terrified to refuse. When he told her to go to the devil, she said she would go to my mother with the story, and so he agreed to pay.

'That was only the first demand, of course, and the price kept going up. When he protested, she taunted him, and pointed out that by agreeing to pay in the first place he'd acknowledged his guilt in the eyes of the world, and that now no one would believe him.'

He got up and started to pace restlessly. 'I love my mother, but she is not a forgiving woman,' he said. 'This would have wrecked their marriage. I came home to Athens for part of my holiday that summer, and I remember how tormented he was. I didn't understand. I thought at first it might be something I'd done to cause him to be so irritable. I was only just fifteen...and I adored my father...' His voice faltered. 'To me, he could do no wrong.'

She said, 'Oh, *darling*!' but he went on as if he had not heard her.

'My God, Jess! Do you have any idea how *helpless* I felt? It was a nightmare. It still haunts me. It scarred me, Jess. That terrible summer left its mark. Finally I persuaded him into telling me what was going on. He lowered his head before saying in a harsh voice, 'My father was a very proud man, but when he told me...he cried. He broke down in front of his young son...can you understand the humiliation he felt? He was a *Greek*. From the Mani! And the Maniot men are very proud. That lying bitch had brought him to his knees.'

'What happened in the end?' she asked.

He took a ragged breath. 'I managed to persuade him to tell his lawyer the whole story. He confronted the girl and threatened to prosecute. She retreated back to her sewer...having taken a tidy sum of money in the meanwhile.'

'But your mother never found out?'

'No, she was spared any pain. My father died a year later. He had suffered from heart problems for some time and,' his mouth grew bitter, 'as far as I'm concerned, he was killed because of two days' folly with a scheming whore.'

'And you thought I was like that?' she said quietly.

'Oh, Jess, forgive me!' He lifted her to her feet and held her tightly. 'Only at the very first...and when Kitty sold the ring. But as soon as you agreed to come to Vathia I knew you weren't.'

'But you still wanted me here—till the ring was paid for.'

'I wanted you *with* me. Damn the ring!' he exploded. 'I'd never met a girl like you in my life before. I couldn't risk losing you. So I...I tricked you, I suppose, into working for me.'

'"O, what a tangled web we weave",' Jess quoted wryly, but he remained serious.

'I'll never trick you again, Jess, I swear it. And you?' He held her away from him so he could look into her eyes. 'No more hiding your true feelings from me. Agreed?'

'Agreed,' she said steadily. 'No more games.'

'Sweetheart!' They stood holding each other for some minutes, then he pulled a strand of her hair through his fingers. 'I love your hair loose,' he said. 'It's like a cape of gold.'

'A pretty untidy cape,' she laughed, taking his comb from his pocket and pulling it through her tousled mane.

She had been deeply moved by his story, her heart wrung with pity for bewildered, fifteen-year-old Andros. What a burden for a young boy to carry! But that was the past, and now the future beckoned, bright with promise. The future! Her heart lifted with joy. She hadn't known such happiness existed. She was so happy, she felt as if she must shine in the darkness like a golden torch!

They ate in the taverna, and tonight she didn't mind when the old men looked at them knowingly, or

Aphrodite chuckled when Andros held Jess's hand. She was proud to be with her lover. Proud to be his lady.

Andros ordered a bottle of *Zitsa*, a pleasant, sparkling wine. 'A sort of Greek champagne,' he said, 'to celebrate.'

Jess, suddenly remembering that this was her last meal in the taverna said, 'You mean, to celebrate the end of my stay?'

'Idiot girl!' he admonished. 'To celebrate *us*.'

Her mouth lifted in a smile. 'How long are you staying in Athens?'

'Only for a couple of days. To get some order into the office, and give George a hard time.'

'Don't be *too* hard on George, will you?' She was so filled with content, she couldn't bear to think of anyone having a hard time on her account, but Andros's face grew obdurate.

'He caused you pain,' he said. In this mood, she knew he was as stubborn as the devil. No point in arguing. It was a novel sensation, having someone look after her. She suspected she could grow to like it!

By the time they had finished their coffee it was late and Jess realised that she was utterly exhausted. She kept trying to suppress her yawns, nearly dislocating her jaw in the process.

'Bed, young lady,' Andros said authoritatively when they were back in the tower. 'I'll fetch your things down to my room while you wash your face.'

She was so tired that she fell asleep the moment she climbed into the big bed, although she had intended to stay awake until he joined her. She vaguely remembered him climbing in and cradling her close, and then she fell into a dreamless sleep.

When she opened her eyes it was dawn and pencils of early sunlight were poking in through the slotted windows. She turned to find Andros leaning on one elbow, looking down at her, watching her while she slept.

His dark eyes were soft with love. 'Good morning, my darling,' he said. 'You're as beautiful asleep as you are awake. Did you know that?'

She smiled, stretching luxuriously. 'Is it very early?'

'*Very!* Much too early to think about getting up.' He started to gently kiss her shoulders.

This time their lovemaking was leisurely. They took time discovering each other's responses, delighting in the exploration of the other's body—languidly stroking and caressing until again they were swept away on a tidal wave of emotion that left them spent and gasping.

Happily replete, they lay tangled together and slept again . . . and made love again . . . before they finally got up. After a hasty breakfast, Jess flung her clothes into a suitcase, and they started on the drive to Athens.

'It's just as well, my wench,' said Andros as they drove along the coast road. 'It's just as well we shall be apart for forty-eight hours, otherwise we both might topple over in complete exhaustion.'

'Speak for yourself!' teased Jess.

He threw her a quick, happy glance. 'Oh, I do! You see, my lovely, my problem is that when I'm with you I can't stop kissing you, and that leads to all sorts of delicious consequences.'

Jess smiled. She couldn't stop smiling. Her usual panic seemed to have disappeared. She and Andros were good together. Everything was going to be all right. And it wasn't only that Andros was the most marvellous lover, skilful and tender. It was the feeling of *completeness* she had when she was with him. Like the two halves of a semicircle that came together to make the whole.

She had missed her noon plane, but they managed to book her on an afternoon flight. Standing among the sea of tourists, she had a sudden premonition of loneliness at the thought of being away from him for even a few days. 'Will you phone me when you arrive in England?' she asked.

'I'll do better than that, you nitwit! I'll phone you from Athens the minute I've booked myself on a plane, and when you meet me at Gatwick I'll spirit you off to my London house.' He hugged her close. 'And you'd better not have any plans for a while. After two days away from you I'll need a *lot* of loving care.' She leaned against him, feeling the rough raw silk of his jacket against her cheek. 'I have plans I want to discuss with you when we get home,' he said.

She wondered if his plans included marriage, and for the first time since they had become lovers a tremor of that old apprehension cast its shadow. It vanished almost as quickly as it had come, and she drew in her breath, determined not to give way to such weakness. It was *Andros* she was involved with now, and Andros was special. Surely her old fears didn't apply to him?

Her flight was called and he took her in his arms and kissed her very thoroughly, ignoring the smiles of people that surged around them.

'You take care of yourself, my darling,' he said as he walked with her to the barrier, 'I'll see you in two days.' He took her hand. 'Don't forget to miss me.'

Jess was suddenly overcome by a sense of impending disaster. Something awful would happen if she left now! 'Why don't I stay with you in Athens?' she blurted, her hand gripping his sleeve desperately.

'Darling,' he gently loosened her fingers, 'of course you can stay if you want.'

She made an effort to regain her self-control. 'No, I'm being idiotic! I do have things to do at home, and it's only a couple of days, after all.' She laughed shakily. 'Bear with me. Being so happy is a bit hard to get used to.' Because that must be what had made her act in such an uncharacteristic fashion.

The flight was pleasant, for Andros had insisted on booking her first class. Jess had never flown first class before, and she enjoyed it. She enjoyed the dinner that was served on china instead of plastic trays, and the complimentary wine that came in crystal glasses. It was nice to have plenty of room for her long legs, and space for her hand luggage. It would have been nicer if Andros had been sitting in the seat beside her, instead of a hefty American businessman who, to her relief, spent the entire flight engrossed in the *Financial Times*, but there would be other journeys, with Andros at her side.

When they arrived at Gatwick, it was late evening and the sky was the colour of a ripe greengage. It would soon be dark. It was really quite warm, but nevertheless Jess shivered and pulled a jacket out of the jumble of clothes in her suitcase. After the burning heat of the Mani, England's mildness struck chill.

She had to wait a bit for the Brighton train, and when they pulled into the station it was later than she had realised, nearly eleven. She hadn't let the Talbots know she was coming back, having planned to phone from the taverna in Vathia that morning, but the phone there had been out of order. She dragged her case over to the row of telephone boxes against the wall of the station. She was sure the Talbots would still be up, for they never went to bed early, being telly addicts. She was prepared to stay overnight in an hotel, but she knew that if it was at all possible Mrs Talbot would find room for her favourite boarder, so she decided to give it a try. The Talbots boarding-house was home to her, and staying in a strange hotel seemed a bleak alternative to going home.

Mrs Talbot answered the phone on the fourth ring. 'Why, Jess!' She sounded amazed. 'We've been trying to get in touch with you all day.'

Jess's heart gave a nasty jolt. 'Why, is anything wrong?'

'No, no, lovey!' her landlady reassured her. 'Nothing wrong. Only we didn't know how to get hold of you, and . . . er . . . you've got . . .'

Jess heard muffled talking in the background, and Mrs Talbot said, 'Just a minute, Jess,' and then presumably covered the receiver with her hand. When she came back on the line, she said, 'There's a surprise waiting for you. I'm not allowed to say more.' She sniffed disapprovingly. 'Why don't you just pop in a taxi and find out for yourself?' She sounded most peculiar. Something had put a damper on her usual sparkle. 'You just hurry along home, dearie,' she said again before she hung up.

As the taxi bowled along towards Hove, Jess wondered what on earth was going on. Could it be something to do with Andros? No, that wasn't possible. Mrs Talbot didn't know about him and, if he had called from Athens to see if Jess had got back safely, it wouldn't affect Mrs Talbot one way or the other. A small knot of anxiety started in her stomach.

When the taxi arrived, she hastily paid the driver and opened the front door. The lights to the Talbots' living-room were on, but the television set wasn't. The only time it was silent was when it was broken, or on the rare occasions that the Talbots entertained. And even then it was usually only turned down to a burbling hum. The knot in her tummy tightened. She only hoped that Mr Talbot wasn't ill.

But before she had a chance to knock on the Talbots' door it opened and Mrs Talbot stood in the doorway. Jess could make out her husband, sitting glumly in his usual chair in front of the blank TV screen. There was another person there, too, sitting just out of Jess's line of vision.

'Oh, Jess! How lovely, you're back!' Mrs Talbot said, and Jess had the feeling that her landlady's nerves—never a problem before—were frayed. 'You'll never guess who's come to visit you!' she said with false heartiness.

At that moment, the figure in the background got up and joined Mrs Talbot at the doorway.

'At last!' said Angela crossly, and Jess discovered herself looking straight into her mother's tear-stained face.

CHAPTER TEN

'MY PRECIOUS baby!' cried Angela, and Jess's heart plummeted, for her mother only called her 'baby' when she was in the midst of a crisis.

She kissed Angela's cheek. 'Hello, Mum! I didn't expect to find you here.'

'I left America very suddenly,' Angela said tightly. 'Where on earth have you *been*, Jess? I've been trying to get in touch with you all day.'

'I've been travelling, mostly,' replied Jess, and then she asked after her stepfather.

Angela coloured and snapped, 'That *brute*! I've left him, Jess.' Her eyes filled with tears.

'P'raps you and your mum would like to come into the kitchen, Jess,' Mrs Talbot suggested, 'and I'll make us all a nice cup of tea. Then Dad can watch his telly.'

Jess felt sympathy for the Talbots. Knowing Angela's habit of constantly complaining when her life was in turmoil, she could imagine the sort of evening they'd had, with poor old Bert Talbot being deprived of his television while Angela regaled them with the story of her life.

In the kitchen, Jess helped to make tea while her mother sat at the table glaring at her daughter. 'I do think, Jess,' she said indignantly, 'that you might have left a phone number where you could have been reached. You knew that I was having difficulties with Elmer.'

What's special about *that*? thought Jess. Angela was always having difficulties with her husbands. She explained that the phone at the taverna had been out of order and her mother snorted, 'Good grief! Didn't that man you were working for have a phone?'

Jess allowed herself a faint smile. 'Phones are a luxury in Vathia,' she said. 'We considered ourselves fortunate to have running water.'

'I can't imagine why you'd want to bury yourself in such a place,' her mother said irritably. 'You must be mad!'

Mrs Talbot slammed the teapot down hard. 'I've put your mum in the big front bedsitter,' she said grimly. 'You can share it with her till your own room's free again.'

Jess agreed and suggested that they take their tea upstairs with them now, and her landlady brightened visibly.

'And get straight to bed, Jess,' she advised. 'You look proper done in.'

Angela got up, fretfully pulling at the silk scarf round her throat. 'I don't know about *Jess* being done in,' she said, '*I'm* exhausted. I haven't slept for thirty-six hours.'

'Then I'd have a bit of a lie-in in the morning if I was you, Mrs Newton,' said Mrs Talbot, making for her living-room and the muffled sound of the television set. 'I'll say goodnight, then. Sleep tight. Don't let the bedbugs bite!'

'Common woman!' Angela muttered as they climbed the stairs to the front bedroom.

Jess, who was still in shock from finding her mother on her doorstep, snapped back, 'She's very kind, Mum. Leave her alone!'

Her mother may have been exhausted, but she didn't go to sleep for a long time. Not until she had told Jess the full details of her last fight with her husband, crying extravagantly over the many cruel things that he had said to her, the unfairness of life in general . . . and *her* life in particular.

Eventually, Jess managed to coax her to put the light out and climb into one of the twin beds, but even then Angela re-hashed the whole business, and it was nearly four a.m. when she finally dropped off to sleep.

Jess lay in the dark, listening to her mother's regular breathing. She was exhausted, for it had been a very long day. Besides, Angela demanded so much sympathy, so much attention, her company always left Jess drained with the effort of bolstering her morale.

She tried to recall last night in Andros's arms, when she had felt so loved, so protected—but the contrast between last night and now was too depressing and she gave it up. She prayed hard that Andros would phone her tomorrow—or rather today—for already it was dawn and grey light was creeping through the curtains.

Telling herself that soon she would see him again and everything would be all right, she drifted off to sleep and dreamt that she was back in the tower, but she couldn't find Andros because Angela had sent him to Wisconsin to live with Elmer Newton...

They slept late and then they went out to buy milk and eggs for breakfast, for there was a small fridge and hotplate in their room. It was a windy day of mixed sunshine and cloud, and Jess suggested a walk on the front.

'Do us good,' she said. 'It'll help to blow away your jet-lag.'

Reluctantly her mother agreed, and they set out briskly for half a mile or so; then Angela started to lag behind. 'I can't go another step.' She sat down in one of the shelters that faced the sea. 'I'm worn out.'

Jess bought them both an ice-cream and then sat on a bench, looking at the grey sea, wondering what Andros was doing in steamy Athens at this moment, anxious that he might phone before she got back.

Angela threw most of her cone into the waste-basket beside the railing. 'I can't finish it,' she said mournfully.

'My stomach has been so upset lately. It's the stress, I've no appetite at all.'

She hunched into the smart American jacket she was wearing and frowned at the pebbly beach. She and her daughter were superficially alike. Their faces were the same shape, and they both had the same grey eyes, but Angela's were dim with disappointment, and her mouth had a discontented droop. Although she was only forty-four years old, her face was already permanently marked with lines of bitterness.

'Do you plan to stay a while in England, Mum?' For, although Angela had not been explicit in her complaints against her husband, she had not said anything about her plans.

She set her mouth resentfully. 'I'm not going back to Wisconsin, Jess,' she said. 'I'm not going back to that man.'

Jess finished her ice-cream before venturing, 'Are you sure you've really given it a chance, darling? I thought you were so happy with Elmer.'

Her mother's eyes flooded with tears. 'Oh, Jess! I was at first. It was the most wonderful love-affair...' She blew her nose into a lace-edged hankie. 'Of course, it changed as soon as we got married. It was like living with a different man.' She clenched her hands. 'You have no idea how they change when you marry them,' she said bitterly. 'Until they've hooked you, they're sweetness itself. Why, Elmer would have walked through *fire* for me before we were married! But once he got that ring on my finger and dumped me in that ghastly house of his...' Words seemed to fail her and she stared moodily at the sea.

'But you said you liked the house,' Jess reminded her.

Angela turned on her petulantly. 'At the beginning, I didn't mind it. I made an *effort* to like it. But it didn't make any difference. He never appreciated how hard I was trying. And he used to leave me alone for *hours*. The only people who visited us were his awful relatives. You have no *idea* what I went through.'

Jess knew from long experience that it was useless to point out that her stepfather was a busy man with a business to run who couldn't always be at his wife's beck and call. She was genuinely sorry for Elmer. She could imagine what the past few months had been like for him.

When they got back, Mrs Talbot met them in the hall. 'You hadn't left the house five minutes but what there was a telephone call for you, she said.

Jess felt the life coming back into her heart. 'For me?' she asked.

'For your mum. From America. He left a number. Said you were to call—"collect"—whatever that means.'

'It means "reverse the charges",' said Angela, taking the piece of paper Mrs Talbot handed her and tearing it in two. 'From your stepfather,' she said grandly to Jess. 'He can call me till he's blue in the face. I won't speak to him.'

After she'd gone upstairs, Jess told her landlady that she was expecting a call from Greece. 'And I take it you *will* be answering it,' said Mrs Talbot drily.

Jess smiled. 'I will.'

'She's ever so bitter, isn't she?' Mrs Talbot said. 'He must have led her quite a dance.'

'He wasn't so bad,' said Jess, and then, because she didn't want to seem disloyal, 'I think she was homesick.'

She spent the rest of the afternoon going through the phone book with her mother, looking for a solicitor, because Angela was determined to get a divorce.

'I won't go back to that life, Jess,' she kept saying. 'Not even if I have to scrub floors to keep myself.'

'You won't have to do that, Mum,' Jess promised wryly, for Angela had never worked a day in her life.

All the time Jess was looking up names and numbers she was waiting to hear the phone downstairs in the hall. But when it did finally ring and Mrs Talbot yelled, 'For you, Jess, Greece!' she found she was loath to answer it. She couldn't understand her reaction. it was very confusing, because she longed for Andros with every breath she drew... and yet she dreaded speaking to him for fear that something would go wrong. Having been closeted for several hours with Angela, listening to her tales of woe, she was beginning to doubt her own judgement and so she answered Andros's, 'How are you, my darling?' in a very subdued manner.

'I'm arriving at Gatwick tomorrow at three,' he said. 'I can't *wait* to see you!'

A strange panic gripped her. For some reason, hearing Andros's mellow voice at the end of the line seemed to put more distance between them than ever.

'I...I'm not sure I can make it,' she said.

'What do you *mean*, you can't make it?' She remembered that tone. It was as abrupt as a slap and it meant he was annoyed.

'Well, it's just...' She was about to tell him that her mother had arrived unexpectedly, but thought better of it. It was hardly a reason for not going to meet him. Angela wasn't an invalid. Besides, he would probably suggest that she brought Angela along, and that was unthinkable! She could just imagine the damper her mother would put on the reunion. In her present mood, she was bound to be hostile to any man who was interested in her daughter. So, 'I—er—I've got a lot to do here,' Jess said lamely.

'Is something wrong, Jess?' he asked sharply.

'Nothing, really, well... nothing serious,' she replied.

'Then you'll be at the airport to meet me?'

'Yes, all right.' Perhaps when she saw him everything would fall into place and this hateful panic would disappear.

'*That's* better!'

Oh, Andros, help me! Help me! her heart cried suddenly.

'I hate being so far away from you, darling,' he said. 'I want to kiss you till you beg for mercy!'

'Do you?' That was inadequate, but it was all she could manage.

He said again, 'Jess, what *is* the matter with you? You sound...different.'

'This is a rather public phone.' It was true that Mrs Talbot had left the door to her living-room ajar.

'Who gives a damn about *that*?'

'Well, *I* do, actually,' said Jess. 'Anyway, I'm not very good on phones. Sorry.'

'Never mind. Tomorrow I'll hold you in my arms and everything will be all right again.'

She muttered half-heartedly, 'Of course.'

'You're certainly *not* good on phones,' he said. 'I think I'll save the rest of my news until I see you. Three o'clock! Don't forget.' And she promised she wouldn't— and hung up first.

She felt utterly miserable. Why was she such a fool? She'd been *longing* to talk to him, and when he had called she must have sounded as if she couldn't have cared less.

She felt trapped by her mother's discontentment, but she also felt powerless to free herself. That was the scary part. With a troubled heart she trailed back upstairs to Angela.

The following day the Sussex coast was deluged with a steady, slanting rain. The iron-grey skies seemed to almost touch the sea, which was the same dull hue. When Jess left for Gatwick she was bundled in her blue raincoat, rubber boots, and a borrowed umbrella. The weather matched her mood, and she sloshed from the bus to the station doggedly. She had thought of nothing but Andros since his phone call. She knew without a doubt that she was deeply in love for the first—and possibly the last time in her life. And now she was *terrified*!

It was Angela who had sparked off her terror. Last night her mother had again wept bitterly about her ruined marriage, her blighted hopes. Jess now firmly believed that her mother had once felt about Elmer the way *she* felt about Andros. She could imagine what anguish she would suffer if the love she felt turned to dislike. The very thought was unbearable.

She tried telling herself that Andros was different. That he inhabited a different world. But surely that could prove to be a disaster too. True, she had shared his world briefly, but now she had returned to reality. A reality of bedsitting-rooms, scratch meals concocted on hotplates, and an unhappy mother. It would have been lovely to have stayed in Andros's world, but she mustn't let herself be trapped by love, the way her mother had so often been trapped. So, after a sleepless night, she came to the desperate conclusion that it would be better to send Andros away. End it, before it turned to ashes.

The plane from Athens was delayed by half an hour and Jess paced up and down the Arrivals hall feeling sick with misery. When the flight was finally announced she stood, tense and white-faced, by a deserted ticket counter.

He was the first through Customs. Tall and straight in a dark business suit, his hair freshly cut and trimmed, his eyes ranged the hall looking for her. She waved briefly from her corner and he came swiftly over to her and took her in his arms. Her iron resolve nearly gave way then, but she forced herself to push him away. He looked down at her in surprise.

'Your briefcase...it's digging into my back,' she said by way of explanation.

'Sorry!' Andros put it on the empty counter. 'Where's your luggage, darling?' he asked.

'I haven't got any.' She focused her eyes on a point somewhere between his collar and the shoulder of his jacket.

'But you know I want to take you home with me. Show you my house.' He went to ruffle her hair and she flinched away from him. 'Never mind! We'll buy what you need. We'll have a shopping spree.'

'I'm not coming with you to London,' she said firmly.

'Darling! Why not? I thought we'd arranged it.'

'*You* arranged it.'

He stopped smiling. 'I'm sorry, Jess. I don't mean to make decisions for you, but I very much want you to come to London with me. I want you to see my home before I...ask you a question.'

'I can't come to your home, now or—or ever, Andros,' she said, turning away to stare at the crowds who jostled her to look at him.

'What are you talking about? What is all this?'

'I'm trying to tell you...' She bit her lips. 'I don't...I *can't* see you any more.'

'Have you gone stark raving mad?' He shook her angrily.

'Let go of me!' she cried, twisting out of his grasp. It helped to take refuge in anger. 'I'm trying to tell you to—to leave me alone. We had a lovely time and—and now it's over.'

His eyes were as hard as jet. ' *"Had a lovely time!"* Is that all it meant to you?'

She gave a faltering laugh. 'You know what they say about holiday romances,' she said.

His lips thinned. 'I don't. Enlighten me.'

'Don't be difficult, Andros.' The pain of unshed tears in her throat was almost unbearable, but she swallowed and went on. 'We had a—a lovely time together in the Mani, but that was Greece. Now we're back in England and things are different.'

He grasped her arms again, bruising her flesh. 'What *things*?' he snarled. 'What the hell are you talking about? Is there another man? Your sailor friend. Is that it?'

Tony! He belonged to another age—another lifetime! She shook her head numbly. 'No...there's no other man.'

'I want to marry you, Jess,' he said, 'I want you for my wife.'

'Well, you know me,' she answered, in a dreadful parody of facetiousness, 'I'm not the marrying kind.'

'What kind are you?' he asked harshly. 'The "one-night stand" kind?'

If he'd stabbed her with a blunt knife he couldn't have hurt her more, and she lashed out without thinking, 'You bastard!'

'I hardly think you're in a position to call me names,' he said coldly.

'Please, Andros...it wasn't like that,' she pleaded through pale lips, 'only...it's never wise to prolong holiday romances...'

'You always had a vulgar streak, Jess,' he grated, letting go of her arms at last and picking up his briefcase. When he faced her again she was shocked by the pain in his eyes. 'I didn't realise that what we had was merely a "holiday romance". I suppose that was my first big mistake.' He squared his shoulders. 'Well, as they say in the films...it's been nice knowing you.'

She watched his tall figure as he elbowed his way through the crowd, out of the building, and she felt as if her heart was being torn from her body.

She wasn't sure how long she waited; it seemed an eternity before she stumbled out to the station to catch her train. When it arrived, she locked herself in the Ladies and leaned against the grimy wash-basin while her body shook with great racking sobs.

When the train arrived at Brighton station she decided to walk to Hove. It wasn't very far, and she needed time to recover from her passion of weeping. She was glad it was still raining with a fierce east wind that cut through her light mac, she could use the rain and wind as an excuse for her bedraggled appearance.

She need not have worried. Angela didn't notice anything wrong, she was much too absorbed with herself to pay any attention to her daughter's red eyes. After a supper of baked beans, which Jess hardly touched, Angela wrote endless letters to English friends, telling them of her return. Jess, who had pleaded a headache, lay on her bed with her eyes closed, trying to come to terms with the feelings of winter that seemed to have closed about her heart.

The next day Jess went job-hunting, although they could have managed quite well for a few weeks on the money she had earned in Vathia. But work was the only therapy that would help her through the next few weeks. If she spent another day closeted with her mother, she would throw her off the Palace Pier! Already this morning she and Angela had had a blazing row.

Angela had decided to return to the Midlands and she was furious because Jess refused to leave Sussex and go with her. 'A *real* daughter would want to live with her mother in her hour of need,' she had screeched, 'not moulder away in some seaside boarding-house!'

'I don't intend to moulder,' Jess had pointed out, 'I want to take a course in business management, so I can get a better job.'

Γ⸱t Angela had refused to understand and had wound up screaming that her only child was yet another disappointment in her life.

'One day you'll be alone, and then you'll know how it feels,' she'd yelled down the stairs as Jess made her escape.

And Jess had muttered, 'I know already,' under her breath.

She visited The Saracen's Head first, to say hello to Ann and Ted Purvis. They greeted her warmly. Her old job had gone, but when they heard of her plans to go back to school Ted offered her a part-time job. 'The regulars still ask after you,' he said. 'They'll be pleased as punch to see you again.'

After Ted had left to attend to some work in his office, Jess had a cup of coffee in the kitchen with Ann.

'You look a bit peaky, Jess,' Ann said, pouring herself a large glass of milk.

'Too much fast living,' Jess joked. She hoped Ann wasn't going to be too tender-hearted. She found that she could cope perfectly well if everything was treated as a joke. It was when people got sympathetic that she had problems. Only this morning Mrs Talbot had said that she and her husband were worried about her, and Jess had been forced to turn away in order to hide a sudden rush of tears.

'I may be looking bad, but you're positively blooming,' she told Ann now.

'Fat, you mean,' Ann grinned. 'Heaven knows what I'll be like in six months!'

Jess looked up from stirring her coffee. 'Are you...?' Ann nodded happily. 'Ann, how wonderful! You must be thrilled.' Jess knew that her ex-boss and his wife had longed for children. 'When's the big day?'

'Not for six months yet. I don't know if poor old Ted will be able to stay the course!' She chuckled. 'His morning sickness is a hundred times worse than mine. At this rate, he's in for a terrible labour!'

'I'm very happy for you both,' said Jess sincerely. 'You can count on me for a babysitter.' And when Ted came back he accepted Jess's congratulations with a beaming smile.

'Isn't she marvellous?' he said, patting his wife's tummy. 'Such a clever girl!'

Ann giggled delightedly, 'I didn't do it by myself, you daft thing.'

'I always understood it was a joint effort,' Jess teased.

She looked at the two of them. At Ann, sipping her milk with a radiant face, and Ted, who seemed about to burst with pride, and she felt a small twinge of envy. Not that she begrudged the Purvises their happiness, but she couldn't help feeling forlorn. Their joy was such a sharp contrast to her own desolate future.

When she'd finished her coffee she went to the college and registered for her course. By then it was lunch time and she decided to look up an old girl-friend who worked in a dress shop in Brighton, and see if they could lunch together. The sooner she made contact with her old friends the better; at all costs, she mustn't allow herself to brood.

Her friend was delighted to see her, and the two girls went to a nearby cafeteria for a sandwich. If Jess had hoped that this lunch date would relieve her feeling of emptiness, then she was disappointed, for she still felt as if there was a glass wall between herself and the rest of the world. She smiled and nodded from behind it, but was as cut off as if it had been made of stone. Fortunately her friend was a chatterbox and didn't appear to notice her silence.

After lunch, the girl returned to work and Jess reluctantly set off for home. She wondered what sort of reception she'd get from Angela. A sulky one, most likely.

It would probably be days before her mother forgave her for staying in Brighton.

She walked home along the front. At least her broken heart was instrumental in providing her with plenty of exercise! The rain had stopped at last, but the sky was still grey, streaked here and there with a livid slash of yellow light, as if the sun was thrusting a knife through the clouds, and the wind whipped the sea into waves that were shaped like small pyramids crested with foam.

Pulling the scarf off her head she let her gold-brown hair loose, and the wind whipped it back off her face. Gulls wheeled and cried. They sounded like fractious babies, and this reminded her once more of Ted and Ann.

It was great that at last they were to be blessed with a child. They'd been married for ten years and had always wanted a family. And they would be super parents. They were still so much in love, the warmth they felt for each other touched everyone who came near them. A child couldn't help but be happy around them.

That was one in the eye for Angela, thought Jess. The Purvises certainly seemed to have survived the delusion of first love. And, now that she thought about it, Mr and Mrs Talbot were a contented and happy couple, and they had weathered forty years of matrimony!

Maybe love didn't change when you married. Or, if it did, it didn't necessarily change for the worse. Perhaps she'd been mistaken all this time. Wasn't it possible that she'd been so brainwashed that she'd only seen the *disasters*? There were plenty of those, of course—but when she came to think about it there was plenty of successes, too. You had to *work* at any relationship; even a friendship required that. Her mother had never been willing to put in that kind of effort. She had only wanted the heady romance, not the solid foundation of a secure love that two people build slowly, over the years together.

The clouds parted briefly and for a moment the gray sea turned to diamonds. Jess pushed her hands down into the pockets of her mac. Maybe it wasn't too late for her. Maybe she could still heal the wounds she had inflicted on herself and Andros. Surely it was worth a try! After all, it was her future happiness that was at stake. It was her *life*!

She would write to him. She would write, and pray that he didn't tear up the letter unread. And, if he ignored it, she'd go to his office and sit at his door until he was forced to see her, to hear her out. She lifted her eyes from the ground and set off briskly, already feeling more alive than she had in twenty-four hours.

She was in such a hurry that when she reached home she didn't notice the taupe-coloured Rolls-Royce standing by the kerb. Her first thought was to get pen and paper, and she bounded upstairs and flung open the door of their room.

Andros was standing by the window. She stood, rooted to the spot. She'd read once that when you were in love you sometimes imagined you saw your lover, only to find it was an illusion, and for a moment she wondered if she was suffering from such an illusion now.

'Hello, Jess,' he said. His face was drawn, and he seemed to have aged since yesterday.

'I was g-going to write to you,' she whispered. 'I couldn't bear it any longer.' And then she was in his arms, crying, laughing, unable to believe this miracle. She felt like a fragile sail-boat that has been tossed by a storm and has come at last to a safe harbour.

'A touching scene!' said Angela from the armchair. Jess had forgotten about her. She had forgotten everything in the wonder of seeing Andros again.

Her mother got up and came towards them. 'Now I understand why you won't come north with me,' she said, and her face was pinched with anger. 'It would have been nice if you'd had the courtesy to tell me the real reason, Jess, instead of that rigmarole about a business management course.'

'I wasn't lying,' Jess said quietly. 'I don't want to live with you, Mum.'

'Because of this man,' Angela insisted.

Jess withdrew from the protection of Andros's arms and faced her. 'Because you're a bitter woman and, if I stay with you, you'll ruin my life. I'm sorry, Mother,' she said gently, 'but that's the way it is.'

'If anybody's going to ruin your life, it will be some *man*!' cried her mother desperately, but Jess refused to listen.

'I've heard it all before, darling,' she said firmly, 'and I don't believe it any more.' She held out her hand to Andros. 'Shall we go out for a bit? There's nothing more to say here.'

They didn't speak until they reached the front, then he guided her to one of the shelters that faced the sea and they sat down. He put his arm around her, and she laid her head on his shoulder. She was still dazed with joy. But it was more than that: those few brief words with Angela just now seemed to have freed her from a great weight she'd been carrying around for years. No matter what the future might bring, she was pretty sure that she would never again feel that sickening sense of foreboding at the thought of an emotional commitment.

'I'm so sorry that I said all those things to you yesterday, Andros,' she whispered. 'None of it was true. But being with my mother again . . . I got into a panic . . .'

'It's all right, darling. I've met your mother and I understand now.' He brushed her cheek with his lips.

'I've been such a fool,' she said.

'Yes, you have,' he hugged her closer, 'but that's all in the past.'

'You came looking for me,' she said wonderingly. 'It's more than I dared to hope for.'

He took both her hands in his and said, 'After I left you yesterday I plunged straight into hell, Jess. You are the breath of life to me. I can't live without you, it's as simple as that. I faced that fact this morning. I'll *teach* you to love me. I'll love you so much, you won't be able to help yourself.'

'Oh, Andros!' She held his hand against her face. 'I've loved you for such a long time! It's just that I was scared...'

'Marry me, Jess. Please marry me, and I'll spend the rest of my life proving to you that marriage can be happy.'

The pale English sun suddenly seemed as vivid as the sun of the Mani. 'Yes. Oh, yes! There's nothing in the world I want more than that!'

'Sweetheart!' He kissed her mouth, her cheeks...then, taking a small jeweller's box from his pocket, he opened it and showed it to her. A large square-cut emerald surrounded by diamonds glittered against the black velvet.

'The Kalimantis engagement ring!' she breathed.

'I've been carrying it around ever since I redeemed it. Wondering when I'd get a chance to put it on your finger.'

'But your aunt...doesn't she want it back?'

He smiled, 'I told her I was thinking of getting married, so she had no choice but to let me keep it with her blessing.'

'Way back then?'

'Way back then.' He slipped it on the third finger of her left hand. 'And there it stays...until the first of our sons marries.'

'Our sons!' She gave a shaky laugh. 'And daughters, too, I hope.'

'Oh, yes! Daughters, too. But not right away. I want you all to myself for a couple of years. And now, darling, I'm taking you home with me to London.'

'What shall I do about my business course?' she asked. 'I registered today.'

'Take the same course in London,' he suggested, 'and then join the family firm.'

'You're serious?'

'Quite serious. I can use a good business partner—and we work well together—remember?'

She laughed aloud. 'I remember!'

'Tomorrow we'll drive down to Shropshire,' he told her. 'My mama's dying to meet you.'

'How does she know about me?' asked Jess suspiciously.

'I phoned her before I drove down here. Told her I'd decided on my future wife.'

'You didn't even know I'd say yes.'

'I didn't care whether you did or not,' he replied. 'I was quite prepared to drug and kidnap you if necessary.'

'That's what I love about you,' she chuckled, 'your powers of persuasion.'

He pulled her to her feet and held her fiercely. 'I'm taking you back to your bedsitter just long enough for you to pack a bag,' he said, 'and then, when I get you in my arms...in my bed...you'll see just how per- suasive I can be.'

Desire stirred in her, a promise of warm, ripe pleasure, and when he kissed her she clung to him, for her legs were weak with longing.

'Let's get married as soon as we can,' he murmured.

She could feel his heart beating a wild tattoo which matched her own. 'Yes,' she agreed fervently. 'Yes.!'

'Would you like to honeymoon in Greece?' He smoothed the hair back from her face. 'Explore the Peloponnese?'

'We could go to Vathia,' she suggested, her eyes shining. 'Fix up a stove in the tower.'

'What romantic ideas you do have!'

'We could sleep on the roof...look at the stars,' she said.

'I'd rather look into your eyes than all the stars in heaven. Come along, my darling.' He tucked her arm firmly in his and they walked back towards the town. 'We've got a lot of lost time to make up for.' And Jess could have sworn that a rainbow arched over them, lighting their way, spilling its colour like a magic carpet along their path.

Harlequin Historicals

Step into a world of pulsing adventure, gripping emotion and lush sensuality with these evocative love stories penned by today's best-selling authors in the highest romantic tradition. Pursuing their passionate dreams against a backdrop of the past's most colorful and dramatic moments, our vibrant heroines and dashing heroes will make history come alive for you.

Watch for two new Harlequin Historicals each month, available wherever Harlequin books are sold. History was never so much fun—you won't want to miss a single moment!

 **Harlequin Romance**

Coming Next Month

2947 BENEATH WIMMERA SKIES Kerry Allyne
Mallory is tired of her international jet-set modeling career and
wants only to manage the outback ranch where she grew up.
Unfortunately, Bren Dalton, the man with the say-so, doesn't think
Mallory capable of it.

2948 SEND ME NO FLOWERS Katherine Arthur
Samantha has doubts about ghostwriting Mark Westland's memoirs,
despite the elderly actor's charm. And when it brings Blaize
Leighton to her door, determined to keep his mother's name out of
the book, her life becomes suddenly complicated....

2949 THE DIAMOND TRAP Bethany Campbell
A schoolteacher's life is thrown off balance when she chaperones a
young music prodigy to Nashville—and falls for the very man she
came to protect her student from! And what about her fiancé back
home?

2950 YOU CAN LOVE A STRANGER Charlotte Lamb
Late-night radio disc jockey Maddie enjoys her life in the quiet
seaside town—until Zachary Nash, a stranger with an intriguing
velvety voice, involves her in a tangle of emotional relationships
that turn her life upside down!

2951 STRICTLY BUSINESS Leigh Michaels
Gianna West and Blake Whittaker, friends from childhood, now
senior partners in a cosmetics company, have known each other too
long to cherish romantic notions about each other. Or so Gianna
believes—until a glamorous rival causes a change of mind...and
heart.

2952 COLOUR THE SKY RED Annabel Murray
As a writer of horror stories, Teale Munro works very unsocial
hours, and he assumes Briony, as an artist, will understand why he
feels able to offer her only an affair. Except that he badly misjudges
Briony and her feelings....

Available in December wherever paperback books are sold,
or through Harlequin Reader Service:

In the U.S.
901 Fuhrmann Blvd.
P.O. Box 1397
Buffalo, N.Y. 14240-1397

In Canada
P.O. Box 603
Fort Erie, Ontario
L2A 5X3

Harlequin Romance

Harlequin American Romance

Romances that go one step farther...
American Romance

Realistic stories involving people you can relate to and care about.

Compelling relationships between the mature men and women of today's world.

Romances that capture the core of genuine emotions between a man and a woman.

Join us each month for four new titles wherever paperback books are sold.
Enter the world of American Romance.

ATTRACTIVE, SPACE SAVING BOOK RACK

Display your most prized novels on this handsome and sturdy book rack. The hand-rubbed walnut finish will blend into your library decor with quiet elegance, providing a practical organizer for your favorite hard-or soft-covered books.

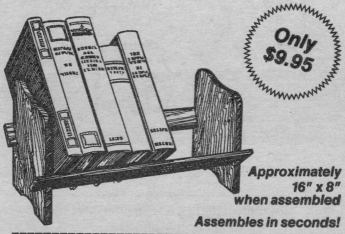

Only $9.95

Approximately 16" x 8" when assembled

Assembles in seconds!

To order, rush your name, address and zip code, along with a check or money order for $10.70* ($9.95 plus 75¢ postage and handling) payable to *Harlequin Reader Service*:

Harlequin Reader Service
Book Rack Offer
901 Fuhrmann Blvd.
P.O. Box 1396
Buffalo, NY 14269-1396

Offer not available in Canada.

*New York and Iowa residents add appropriate sales tax.

BKR-1A